Losing Forever

Losing Forever

by Gayle Friesen

Kids Can Press

Kids Can Press acknowledges the financial support of the Ontario Arts Council, the
Canada Council for the Arts and the Government of Canada, through the BPIDP, for our
publishing activity.

The author wishes to acknowledge the financial support of the Ontario Arts Council in
the writing of this novel.

ONTARIO ARTS COUNCIL
CONSEIL DES ARTS DE L'ONTARIO

Published in Canada by
Kids Can Press Ltd.
29 Birch Avenue
Toronto, ON M4V 1E2

Published in the U.S. by
Kids Can Press Ltd.
2250 Military Road
Tonawanda, NY 14150

www.kidscanpress.com

Edited by Charis Wahl
Designed by Marie Bartholomew
Printed and bound in Canada

CM 02 0 9 8 7 6 5 4 3 2 1
CM PA 02 0 9 8 7 6 5 4 3 2 1

National Library of Canada Cataloguing in Publication Data

Friesen, Gayle
    Losing forever

ISBN 1-55337-031-7 (bound).   ISBN 1-55337-032-5 (pbk.)

    I. Title.

PS8561.R4956L68 2002   jC813'.54   C2001-903444-X

PZ7.F91665Lo 2002

Kids Can Press is a ᶜᵒʳᵘˢ™ Entertainment company

For Bradey and Alex and the Mara gang
with love

ACKNOWLEDGMENTS

I'd like to thank Jennifer Stokes, who knows many things that I do not, for her copyediting and Charis Wahl for editing that truly went above and beyond on this one. I'd also like to thank Brian for his support and my three sisters — Barb, Pat and Bren — for their sisterness.

The water at Mara waits for me. As soon as my foot hits the sun-warmed planks of the dock, I can sense the waiting. I walk to the end of the wharf — feel the movement of the waves beneath me, that slow, gentle rocking. Sometimes I wait for a long time, because I know in a split second it will be over — gone for another entire year. I actually shiver, even on the hottest days.

When I can't wait anymore, I raise my arms to the lost stars. Briefly I am air until my fingertips meet the water that lets me glide like a rainbow — fingers, wrists, elbows and the hot crown of my head. But then it's knees, ankles and toes. I'm always a little sad that I can't feel every inch of myself entering the water. My body follows too quickly to register the movement. But I always feel my feet, because they're last.

Once I'm in the water, that's when I greet her. "I'm back," I whisper. Mara shivers in response. My entry causes ripples to the farthest edges of her shore.

1

"What if Cinderella hadn't been home that day?"

Sam didn't answer. He was busy perfecting his lay-up shot in our backyard.

"Or what if Sleeping Beauty had just rolled over and snoozed for another ten years? Would her prince have waited, kept trying? Didn't she have a real name? She must have had a name. Why can't I remember —"

Sam tossed the ball, hard, in my direction. I held my arms out and deflected it so that it landed in the rosebush. Sam retrieved it quickly, checking the window to make sure Mom wasn't watching.

"What's with the fairy tales?" He threw the ball over his shoulder without looking at the hoop. As if. Missed by a mile. "Let's play. I'll give you a two-point lead."

"Ooh, reverse psychology. That's going to work — my mom's been trying that on me for years."

"Come on."

"It's too hot. What was her name? It's driving me crazy."

"Short trip. You live next door to crazy."

"I live next door to you."

He grinned his lopsided grin, braces gleaming, straw-colored hair hanging over his face like a droopy curtain. He pushed it back, revealing bright green eyes. "Snow White," he said suddenly.

"Huh?"

"That was her name."

I laughed. "Sleeping Beauty's name was Snow White?" Sam could always make me laugh. We'd been friends forever. "Hmm. Actually, Snow White had it pretty good — living in that vine-covered cottage in the woods with her seven little friends. They probably went fishing all the time — swam in the lily pond, partied from dawn to dusk. Why did she trade it in for a boring old life in the castle? What do you want to bet she never even saw the old gang again after she hooked up with her prince? Can you imagine Dopey or Sneezy being invited to a royal ball? Uh-uh. No way."

Sam stretched out his long legs on the deck chair. "What is with the fairy tales?" he asked again, gazing up at the sky, hands hooked behind his head.

"I was just thinking about lies in general. And that whole business of forever — loving someone forever, you know? It's a big, fat fairy tale."

"I'll love you forever." He grinned at me again.

I scowled so that I could actually feel the frown lines digging into my eyebrows. "Why do you say stuff like that?"

"To see you blush." He reached for the camera in the bag beside his chair. Some people carry a rabbit's foot; Sam always has his camera. You never know when a picture might show up, he liked to say. He had a million photo albums at home.

"No pictures," I ordered, and he actually listened. Then I added more quietly, "and I don't blush."

"I know. You're just mad that Dell has a boy-friend this summer."

I grabbed my drink and drained it in one gulp until the ice cubes banged into my teeth. "It's none of my business if she wants to go out with Marshall. Even if he *doesn't* know her middle name."

Sam gasped, flipping over so he landed in a heap on the deck. He kept his face down, flailing his fists against the faded planks. "The pig doesn't know her middle name?" He raised himself onto his elbows and slowly inched his way toward me. "Say it isn't so."

"You're going to get slivers." I looked down at him.

"I'd welcome the pain if it helps me forget that Marshall doesn't know Dell's middle name." He lifted his head and howled. "Jessica Joy Miner-Cooper."

I jumped up at the sound of my own name. Jessica Joy. It sounded like a stuffed animal. And then there's the lying hyphenated last name.

I raced over to the water hose and aimed it at him, ready to fire.

"Jessica Joy — who's never coy," he sang off-key. "She ran away with the next-door boy."

I turned the hose on and managed to drench part of his shirt before he lunged at me.

Despite myself, I screamed and dropped the hose. I'm pretty tough, but I lose it when someone chases me.

I ran across the lawn, and I would have made it in the back door except for two things. One, Mom had just washed the floor and two, Sam had (as Mom-the-therapist would say) no boundaries when it came to winning. I made a last ditch run for the playhouse, but I could feel the spray hitting my legs. I stopped and let it happen. Sam howled with happiness and showed no mercy. Then, being the kind of guy he is, he turned the hose on himself. By now I was giggling helplessly — a girl thing I try to avoid, but there you go.

I grabbed two towels that were drying in the sun and threw one over to him. We spread them out and lay on our backs to dry off.

I could feel the heat of the midday sun spreading itself across me like a blanket.

"See that cloud, that wisp of a cloud that looks like a roof with the outlines of a house beneath it, Jes? That's a vine-covered cottage. We could live there —"

"Uh-huh, Dopey. Until a big storm moves in, right? Then what happens?"

He closed his eyes and raised his chin toward the sun. "You're the least romantic girl I've ever met. It's quite unnatural."

I scrambled to my feet and went to retrieve the basketball. "One on one, Dreamer Boy. And I'll spot *you* two points."

2

I held the receiver at arm's length, but I could still hear Dell's high-pitched, excited voice, even though the words were now reduced to a fuzzy babble. She'd spent the day with Marshall and I'd been listening — good friend that I was — for at least twenty minutes of play-by-play. But when she got to the part where she was naming their future children, I stopped paying attention.

Eventually I could tell there was silence at the other end, so I pulled the receiver quickly back to my ear. "Wow. Sounds like fun."

"I said he sprained his wrist."

"Oh." Busted. "Is he okay?"

"He didn't sprain his wrist. I was checking if you were listening. You were holding the phone away from your ear, weren't you?"

Busted again. She was good; I had to give her that.

"You want to come over tonight?" I asked. "Mom

and Cal are going out to plan some incredibly crucial detail of their wedding, like what color bow tie the caterer should wear. We could order pizza."

"Can't. Marshall's going to show me his baby home videos tonight. You could come."

I mimed a retching gesture with my finger down my throat and it made me feel a bit better.

"Well, that does sound exciting. Or, I could just sit in the lotus position in my bathroom and watch the mold spread across the tile grout."

"One, you don't do yoga. Two, your mother is going to kill you if you don't clean your bathroom and three … why don't you like him?"

Her voice grew smaller on point three and I felt like the same scum she was absolutely right about my mom killing me over. "I do like him. I just don't know him very well. He is totally hot, I'll give you that."

"He is, isn't he?"

"A babe. Baborama. Babalicious."

"Jes."

"No, I mean it. He's cute. But I don't know if I'm ready to see him in diapers yet, okay? Or blowing out the candles on his first birthday cake. Besides, Mom said she's got this big surprise for me and she was all thrilled about it, so I better hang around."

"A surprise?" Dell sounded excited. "What do you think it is — a puppy?"

I laughed. "A puppy. Yeah, can't you just see my mom in her designer suit holding a furry, hair-shedding, squirmy puppy?" I did my best "mom" impression. "'Jes, honey, I know you're not thrilled about getting a stepfather, but here's a puppy ... so we're even, okay?' Yeah, I think you're on to something there."

"So when do you think you're going to get used to the fact that your mother is totally serious about marrying this guy, like, in a month."

"Like, never."

"He's pretty nice, as far as old guys go."

"He's a wiener."

Dell laughed. "All beef or turkey?"

"Turkey."

"Jessica."

"Adele."

"Name one totally bad, horrible thing about him."

"He sucks his teeth, blinks when he's nervous, tries too hard ... way, way too hard ..."

"One thing I said."

"He shaves his legs."

"That's because he's a cyclist."

"I think he likes it."

"You know what I think?"

"Like I could stop you from telling me."

"I think you don't like him because he's not your father."

She was, of course, right.

"Jes?"

"You know what I was thinking the other day, Dell? I was thinking that even though my mother is a psychologist, there probably is still room in my life — in my brain — for another person to go rummaging around. And that what I really, you know, desire is that at some point my brain would just open up and spill out so that anyone with a diploma or a really cool business suit could just go poking around, holding up my thoughts and feelings to the light whenever they wanted so that they could tell me what I'm thinking. Because I really need that, you know? I really am incapable of deciding what I feel and think. So I need all the help I can get. Really."

Silence.

"So you don't want to come over tonight?" she asked calmly.

"Maybe tomorrow. Say hi to Marshall for me."

"One ... two ..."

I heard her say, "Three." And then we both hung up.

Dell and I became friends in grade three. Until then I had mostly hung out with Sam, but he was going through his "girls are yucky" phase and I was stranded. When the teacher had changed the seating arrangement in the classroom, Dell and I were seated next to each other. I admired her curly, red hair because it looked like a campfire and I told her so.

Her eyebrows shot way up and I thought at first I'd insulted her, but she dove for a notepad in her backpack and I saw her scribbling down my compliment word for word. I noticed her "p" was backward.

"That was descriptive," she whispered.

"Good word," I whispered back.

The teacher made us stay in at recess for talking and Dell drilled me with questions as we cleaned the chalk brushes. Where did I live? What was my favorite color? (Hers was fuchsia.) Wasn't *Baseball Ballerina* the best book ever? (I didn't know, but I said I'd read it.) How many brothers and sisters did I have? (She had a very mean sister named Pammy.)

I'd grown silent for a second, but then I told her what I had not yet said out loud to another person. "My sister died."

All of eight years old, she had wrapped her arm around my shoulder. She'd said nothing, but I saw a big tear fall to the floor. Our friendship was forged on chalk dust and a tear.

Now I warmed up the supper Mom had left, such as it was. Leftover (dried out) chicken with soupy mashed potatoes. I pushed the baby carrots to the side — they'd been microwaved into dehydrated toes.

Lately I'd been reading magazines with recipes in them, mostly in the hope that there was something in the world of cuisine that didn't require a can of mushroom soup. Cooking totally mystified my mom. Cooking and — lately — me.

"Why don't you like Cal?" She had asked after our first dinner together. "Why don't you give him a chance? He's a *terrific* guy."

Terrific. Terr-I-fic. That's how she'd said it. Maybe I'd only been around for fifteen years, but I knew suspicious words when I heard them. *Terrific, super, fabulous* — they all set off an alarm inside my brain because they hid another meaning, one not nearly as terrific, super or fabulous. Words that hid a lie. Words like *forever*.

I scraped my plate and put it into the dishwasher.

Mom had brought Cal home six months ago. She'd already been seeing him for a while. They worked at the same counseling group and between the two of them, they knew everything. Their big entertainment was to watch television and analyze body language. Talk shows were their favorite. "See how she's crossing her arms? Defensive. Check out that bouncing foot across the knee. Nervous, anxious." And they'd laugh hilariously. I'd turn up the volume, thinking that maybe the dialogue could actually tell me something.

"So, Jessica, you're in grade nine?" That had been Cal's opening line when he met me.

"Yup."

"You like school?" Highly original.

"It's okay."

"Your mother says you're a whiz in English. You like to read?"

"Yup."

"I never read much in school. Didn't like novels. I prefer true stories."

You know the sound that water makes when the last of it is being sucked down the drain? That was the exact noise I heard in my head when he said that.

"Funny, I always thought fiction was about truth."

Old Cal had looked kind of bemused at that and tipped his head to the right. (Mom always tips hers to the left.) He'd put his finger on his chin and said, "Hmm, that's interesting."

Interesting. Add that to the *terrific, super, fabulous* list. Sounds like one thing. Generally means another.

There was no air moving inside the house, so I went to the backyard. I picked up the basketball and took a shot. It swished through the net neatly. Out of habit, I glanced over to Sam's house, but it was quiet. They'd gone up to the lake for the weekend. Sam had two younger brothers, Henry and Danny, and when they were home, you knew it. Sam pretended his brothers were a pain in the butt, but it wasn't true. He was the best big brother I could imagine. He was always showing them how to do things, like flying a kite or throwing a baseball. We'd known each other since we were babies. Literally. Our moms took us for walks in our carriages together, sent us to swimming lessons and drama camp together. He was my best friend next to Dell.

Sam almost blew it, though, last year. Out of nowhere. We'd gone Rollerblading and I'd swerved to miss a crazed power walker. I'd landed in the bushes and Sam helped me to my feet with a silly smile on his face. Before I could wipe the dirt off my elbow pads, he just did it — grabbed me and kissed me! To be fair, he looked surprised after he'd done it, but he made it worse when he tried to explain.

"You just looked so cute down there ... all rumpled and ... cute."

Cute! I'd exploded. "Don't call me cute!" Ugh. It was not my fault that my parents' genes had conspired to leave me with a shrimpy, five foot practically nothing form that had already threatened to stop growing. I didn't want to be cute. I felt huge inside, like a giant forced to live in a doghouse. I wanted to loom, to fly, to soar above the regular. I wanted to stoop for things, not reach — always looking up into someone's nose hair. I wanted to be the same six feet tall on the outside that I knew I was on the inside.

You're so intense, I could almost hear Dell say.

That was the nice thing about best friends. They hung with you even if they weren't actually there.

I took another shot. It hit the rim and wobbled, then fell away.

I hadn't talked to Sam for two weeks after "the kiss." He tried phoning; I hung up. He'd come over; I'd pretend I wasn't home. Finally he slipped a note under the door with a stick-figure boy holding his decapitated head. "I lost my mind," the caption read. I forgave him then, but he was still on probation.

"Yoo-hoo. We're home." Mom's voice trickled across the backyard. Then I saw her peeking through the back window. She waved me inside — right, the surprise. Dell's theory crossed my mind, but I knew it was a long shot even though I'd been asking for a dog since I was ten.

Still, I felt a twinge of anticipation.

"Honey," Mom met me with a too-tight hug and I could tell she was nervous. Body language. What can I say? You live with a shrink, some of it rubs off.

"I have a big surprise for you."

Crazy thoughts twisted inside me. "Cal and I have broken up." "The wedding's off." "Your father and I are getting back together." Or, at the very least — "Say hello to Rover."

"Okay, Cal," I heard Mom say. "You can bring her in."

Cal walked through the door, grinning like a jack-o'-lantern. Behind him was a girl. Screech and thud. The doggy dream smashed into the wall. I tipped my head to the left. No, not a girl. Somebody's idea of female perfection floated like a hologram into the room. Long, blond, crinkly hair, dazzling green cat eyes, slender and tall. Utter perfection, like she should be running across a beach in slow motion — like she should go everywhere in slow motion.

"You remember I told you Cal had a daughter the same age as you? Angela? Well, here she is."

"Your new sister," Cal said.

I saw Mom bite her lip as soon as these words were uttered. She bit her upper lip and a shadow of remembering crossed her face.

3

I rang the buzzer at Dad's apartment, hoping he'd be home. With his part-time work schedule, he usually was.

"Yeah?" he answered gruffly.

"Hey, Dad. It's me."

"Hey, yourself. Come on up." His voice changed, lightened.

I timed my push to coincide with the buzz. It had taken me at least three visits before mastering it. Now I was an old pro and the door clicked as I pushed.

Making my way through the narrow halls, I tried to ignore the cooking smells. Cabbage and curry. Hope it wasn't the same meal. For the first couple of months after the separation, I'd tried to tell myself it was temporary. Mom and Dad were telling the truth, they needed time to work out their feelings. Dad wouldn't always live inside this beehive with old number four hundred and one, who complained bitterly when the elevator was being used for moving, or number four hundred and seven, who resembled most of the people I'd seen on "Most Wanted" television programs. Dad didn't belong here with other people's problems and clashing cooking smells.

"Jes! What a great surprise."

"Hi, Dad." I gave him a hug and he returned it, kissing the top of my head.

"I wasn't expecting you until tomorrow morning. But I'm not complaining."

"I thought you might be out …"

"Nope. I was just hanging out … doing some reading." He pointed to a thick novel splayed open on the coffee table.

"You should get out more, you know."

"You don't have to worry about me, Funny Face."

I looked around the room, "early ugly" with no pictures on the walls, just cleaner patches of paint where somebody else's art had hung. Somebody else's life.

"How's your mother?" he asked.

"Fine. Good. *Super.* You know Mom."

"Uh-huh," he said.

Stupid. They'd known each other since high school. *You know Mom?* Stupid.

"The wedding plans are all going ahead," I bumbled on. "She's planned every detail to the …"

"Yup, yup. Everything's on track, right?"

I nodded and went over to the small kitchenette. I opened the fridge and pulled out a soda. At the top of the wall, just below the ceiling, some ex-tenant had started stenciling flowers and watering cans in pastel shades of pink and blue. Then, half-way around the teeny-tiny room, they'd stopped. What could have been so important that they couldn't finish a measly job like that? It made me mad.

"Have you had dinner?" Dad asked.

"Not much."

"I was just going to make some stir-fry."

"Sounds great. Can I help?"

"Sure. Chop up the celery and the onions, would you?"

"Not the onions," I groaned. "I'll cry like a baby."

"Better you than me, kiddo." He handed me a knife. "So, you like this Cal guy then?"

A claw reached inside me and gathered up my insides in a fierce grip. The more Dad asked about Mom's life, the more the claw tightened. The more he mentioned her, the more I was sure I could see his heart shining through his faded denim shirt ... pumping blood despite the crooked crack down the middle.

"He's okay. Dad, this celery looks like it's from the last millennium."

"Well now, that's because it's thousand-year-old celery. Very rare, very expensive, very ..."

"Deadly. Look, it doesn't even crunch. It just

sort of bends." I did a visual demonstration, twisting the celery into a pretzel shape.

He peered over my shoulder. "It probably isn't supposed to do that, huh? Come to think of it, these tomatoes are looking a little sickly, too. Guess I was planning to have that stir-fry last week."

I shook my head and put down the wilted celery. "Pizza?"

"Hold the olives."

"Hold the olives? That's the best part. Pizza without olives is like ..."

"Okay, okay. Half with olives. Compromise."

"Compromise."

I punched speed dial number two for Tom's Pizza and wondered fleetingly if many people had a pizza joint on one speed dial and Chinese food on the other.

"So, what brings you here on a Friday night? We're still going fishing tomorrow, aren't we?"

I took a big sip of my soda and nodded. I wondered if I should tell him about Cal's daughter, Angela. I'd known Cal had a daughter, of course. She lived in California with her mother. And I figured she'd come for the wedding, but I hadn't thought she'd show up so soon.

Mom had tried to explain. "We didn't expect her this early either. She just called Cal from the bus station saying that she was here."

"So why doesn't she live with him?"

Mom had hesitated. "His place is so small. Besides, with his work at the group home, he's not even at his apartment some nights. This will give us a chance to get acquainted." But she had an unconvincing grin on her face, like she was trying to talk both of us into a used car that we didn't really need. Then she added casually that Angela would be staying in my room.

That's when I'd thrown a mini-minor conniption.

"My room?"

"Well, I suppose I could empty a closet and put her in there," she'd said crisply, checking out the doorway as if she could see if my voice had carried up the stairway.

"Fine. A closet, the attic ... stick her in a tent in the backyard for all I care. Just not in my room."

Mom had closed the kitchen door firmly, taken a deep breath and slipped into her counseling pose.

"So, what I hear you saying is that you don't want to share your room? Help me to understand that." The timer was on. Our session had begun and I knew right then that the battle was lost. I wouldn't even get to fire a shot.

"Forget about it, Mom. I was just on my way to Dad's. I promised to bring over some, uh, books." Bald-faced lies. All of them.

"But it's Angela's first day! I was hoping we

could get to know each other. I bought an ice-cream cake!"

When my mom and dad split for good, we'd gone out for hot-fudge sundaes. I could see a definite trend building here. I wondered if this approach worked for her suicidal clients. *Hey, I know things look bad ... rocky road or butter pecan?*

"We're going fishing tomorrow, Mom. This way we can get an early start."

She'd agreed, and not as reluctantly as I thought she might. In fact, she'd almost seemed relieved.

"Hey there, space cadet." Dad prodded my shoulder. "Where'd you go?"

"Huh? Oh, nowhere. Did you get that new lure for tomorrow? I thought I'd spend the night if that's okay. We could get an earlier start."

"Fine with me. Are you sure everything's okay? You look, uh, preoccupied."

"Nah. I'm good."

Dad shrugged and flicked on the television. He wouldn't probe.

After the pizza, three shows and a game of backgammon, Dad helped me pull the futon to the floor and make my bed. The faded psychedelic flower sheets were ones I remembered from Mom and Dad's bed when I'd crawl in after a nightmare. In some places the sheets were threadbare, almost worn through. I ran my hands over the spots.

"I guess I should get some new sheets," Dad said.

"No," I said loudly. Too loudly. He seemed surprised. "I like them, Dad. They're cozy, broken in. Don't get new sheets. Promise?"

He straightened, smiling uncertainly.

"Okay, I promise. Cross my heart, hope to die ..."

"Stick a needle in my eye." I finished the old rhyme with him.

I kissed him goodnight and watched as he walked over to his cupboard-size bedroom, picking up the thick novel as he went.

"What are you reading?" I asked.

"Oh, you know me and my dusty Russian novels. Something to put me to sleep."

I smiled, but it faded as he left the room. Sleep was probably hours away for him. He loved those books. Tolstoy, Dostoyevsky — the thicker and more depressing the better. Who knew, maybe it made him feel better to compare tragedies.

I tossed around on the hard futon. I tried to blank out my mind so there'd be nothing left to do but sleep, but it was like somebody kept pressing the rewind button. I hadn't said more than a couple of words to Angela, but I could still see her perfectly, standing in the kitchen behind Cal. The two of them, they were the future. Mom's future. I pulled the familiar blankets up around my chin, closed my eyes tightly and waited for sleep to come.

4

Mara was glossy smooth. Reflected pines fringed the edges, making it look as though there was another world just below the calm surface of turquoise water. I dipped my feet and watched as the ripples altered the illusion. My feet remained totally still until the ripples had drifted away. Then they were part of the underwater forest. I listened for the pair of loons who made their home here, but they were silent today.

I'd been coming up to this lake since I was six months old and it was as familiar to me as me. Maybe even more because it never changed. There were more cabins now and a few less trees as people made room for better views — it made me furious every time — but the lake itself remained the same. And, as usual, it comforted me.

"Hey." Dad's voice called to me from the foot of the dock.

"Hey, yourself," I called back.

"Were you wanting me to load all the gear or would you consider helping?"

"I was thinking you could do it," I called back. He was wearing his goofy "lucky" fishing hat and his forest-green vest with pockets covered with lures and flies and hooks. Mr. Field and Stream.

"Wrongo." The word barked across the still air.

I rose reluctantly and helped him pack everything into the boat. When the last of it was allocated, we settled ourselves into our seats and pushed off. In Mom's space sat the drinks and snacks cooler, promoted from the hull where it used to be.

We baited our hooks once we arrived at our favorite spot and dropped them into the water.

I leaned against a life jacket and stretched out my legs, feeling the warm sun begin to make its way through the morning chill.

"Dishes for twenty," Dad predicted.

"Dishes for, oh, thirty-five," I countered.

"Feeling a little pessimistic today, are we?"

"Realistic."

If the first nibble came within twenty minutes, I'd have to do dishes. If it came within thirty-five minutes, he'd do them. It was a bet we'd been making since I'd learned to tell time.

A thought came to me. "What if people never learned to tell time? When do you think we'd figure it out?"

"Figure what out? How to tell time?" He pushed his hat back so that I could see his blue eyes.

"No." I shook my head. "When do you think we'd realize that eventually it all runs out?"

He sighed. "It's too early for that kind of question. I haven't even had my first cup of coffee. Let me get some caffeine into my system."

Adults and their coffee. Honestly, it was like their brains were on stand-by until that first hit.

"Sorry. Forgot about your addiction," I said.

He unscrewed the Thermos lid and poured the steaming liquid into his chipped cup, the one with a handle like the tail of a salmon.

"I'll remember that when it's time for your four o'clock Slurpee," he shot back.

Oops. One for the parent. I shrugged my defeat. It was true. Four o'clock was Slurpee time, rain or shine. Another tradition. Man, we had a lot of those. It was one of those things Mom had always hated. Or, if not hated, never understood.

"Let's go spend the day hiking," she'd suggest.

"Hiking?" we'd say. "This is a fishing lake."

"Let's go for Chinese tonight."

Chinese? We always cooked trout the first night, or hot dogs if the fish weren't cooperating. Eventually she'd given up trying to change our routine. Well, given up, anyway.

Yeah, Jes. That's why she and Dad split. Because of our lake routines. Even I wasn't that stupid.

I remember when she and Dad sat me down with my hot-fudge sundae for the "big talk." Mom had done most of the talking, as usual. She'd started out with one of her famous "word pictures": marriage was like a road that two people choose to walk together. But sometimes there's a fork in the road and you have to decide which path you're going to follow. Sometimes you end up choosing different paths. I think she went on to mention forests and underbrush and paths leading back to the main road ... but by that time her words filled the air like brown smog, and all I could hear was the sound of my spoon scraping the bottom of the plastic dish.

"Just tell her the truth, Elli," Dad had finally said. He'd sounded frustrated and angry.

Mom had given him a long, hard stare, and they seemed to exchange more truth in that glance than in anything I had heard so far. She'd shaken her head slightly, her mouth drawn in one straight line. Dad had only sighed.

"It's just a separation, sweetie," Mom had said finally. "We need time to sort things out."

I remember looking at their untouched sundaes — the ice cream melting beneath the thick, warm chocolate until it was an oozing, gooey mess like the truth that was right there in front of me. Their marriage had melted away. What was once firm and sure and distinct was now a sodden blob covered in gooey, congealed, empty sweetness.

I never once thought the breakup was my fault. It didn't have anything to do with me because clearly, if they had thought even once about me, they'd still be together.

When the separation turned into divorce proceedings, Mom volunteered to be the assistant coach for my softball team. We were a pretty crappy team and Mom thought there was too much "negative energy" going on. I made her promise not to use that statement on the field.

The other girls liked her because she knew all their names right away and would say nice things about their hair. Plus, every other week or so she'd bring a big box of Fudgsicles to the practice. (The woman has a fetish for ice-cream treats.)

In the final tournament we lost four games in a row, each more devastatingly than the one before. The final game was mercied in the fifth inning. We were all feeling pretty low, especially me since I was pitching most of the games. Mom did her cheerleader thing, whipping out encouraging words left, right and center, but it didn't help.

It was the hottest day of the century and we all slouched afterward in the dugout, slurping at our water bottles. Mom decided to address the team and I knew right away it was going to be a disaster. She started off by saying that life had a way of challenging us in areas we couldn't anticipate. And it wasn't whether we won or lost, it was how we played the game. She actually said this. People groaned.

"No, really," she had continued, undaunted. "I don't want you girls to let this experience define you. This is something that should challenge you. The failure isn't who you are."

Well, nobody had really thought that they were failures. Obviously, the other teams were just way better and we basically sucked. But I knew Mom wasn't talking about softball, and she wasn't talking to the team.

Don't let the divorce define you. That's what she was really saying. I wanted to scream at her not to bring our life out here in the open. But what I really hated was how calm she sounded.

Twenty minutes passed as Dad and I sat in the boat, then the thirty-five minute mark. But at sixty minutes, the fish started biting. By noon we'd filled our quota and we headed back to shore.

"I'll clean if you cook," Dad said.

"You're on." Cleaning the fish always made me sad. Too much reality is never a good thing.

I hopped out of the boat and tied it up. After helping to lug everything back to our little gray cabin nestled in the pines, I announced my intention to go find Sam.

"Sure thing. Quiet on re-entry. I'm going to take a nap."

I waved and headed off to the creek. On the other side of the rushing water was the Little Sparrow campground, where Sam's family had a cabin.

I crossed the creek on the log — "Billy Goat Gruff" bridge, as Sam called it — and scanned the swimming area for the familiar tow-headed family. Every last one of them was blond, even their retriever, Single Malt. He was the first one to see me and, barking excitedly, he raced across the sand.

"Hey, Malty-boy, sweetie-pie, love bug!" I buried my head in his soft, downy fur and scratched his sides. He wiggled all over from stem to stern.

Single Malt. Dumb name for a dog, I thought, but better than Pale Ale, which was what Sam's mom, Amber, wanted to call him.

"It's Jes!" I heard a squeaky voice yell from the beach. I looked up in time to see Danny running toward me, covered from head to toe with gritty remnants of his sand castle.

He hurled himself, all arms and legs and ears, at my chest. Bright blue eyes peered up at me through dirty blond bangs. He was cuter than cute times ten. I hugged him back.

"Where did you get that bruise, Danny Boy, the pipes, the pipes are calling?"

"Oh, man." He let go as suddenly as he had taken hold and pulled up a sleeve to reveal all its glory. "Look at this." A big purple and yellow bruise the size of a potato stared up at me.

"What happened?" I sat down on the sand.

"Well, it was like this." He plopped down beside me, close enough so that I could smell his little-boy sweat, like freshly shucked peas. "We was building a fort at the creek and Henry picked up this big rock." Danny stretched his arms to indicate a rock slab large enough to cover the mouth of a small cave.

"Wow, that Henry is strong," I observed.

Danny nodded solemnly. "Not strong so it wouldn't fall, though. And I was helpin' so it wouldn't, but then it did. Right on my arm."

"That must have hurt."

"Oh, man."

"How's the rock?"

"George? He's okay."

Most of the inanimate objects at the Schmidt household had names. The car was Vicky Volvo, the house was Homer. Right down to specific flowers and shrubs. Everything was granted living status and I envied it far more than I would admit.

"Hey, Pigtails. How's it going?" Sam's dad, Geoff, ambled up beside me, long and rangy like the caraganas grass that grew all over this place.

"Maybe you hadn't noticed that I cut them off last year," I said, touching my short hair with one hand.

"I noticed. Saddest day of my life." He grinned down at me.

"You have a good life if that was your saddest day."

"I'm not complaining. Your dad up at the cabin?"

"Yup. But I think he's taking a nap."

"A nap! He's far too young to be napping the day away."

There was an awkward pause as both of us knew he'd only taken up napping since the divorce or, as Sam called it, the Great Divide.

"I think I'll wander over there," he said, and I nodded, suddenly warm with gratitude. Back home, Mom had custody of the Schmidts as neighbors, but at the lake, Dad had visitation rights.

"You help with my castle, 'kay, Jes?"

"'Kay, Danny Boy, the ..."

"... pipes, the pipes are calling," he sang off-key as he raced toward the masterpiece that was crumbling in the hot summer sun.

As I got up to join him, Geoff put his big hand on my shoulder. "You doin' okay, Pigtails?"

Tears burned suddenly and unexpectedly in my eyes. I blinked them away furiously. "I'm fine," I said. "I better help Danny before the whole thing falls apart."

I was up to my armpits in clay and sand by the time Sam ambled down to the water's edge.

"Don't wreck it, Sam," Danny warned.

Sam lifted a foot and let it hover above the newly formed turrets I'd painstakingly put in place.

"One small step for man ..."

"One small step and you're a dead man," I warned.

"Sammy!" Danny howled.

"Relax, Shrimp." Sam hauled his Sasquatch foot back to safer ground. He slumped down and lay back on the sand, shading his eyes from the sun.

"You're up early today," I remarked. "It isn't even sunset."

"Catch any fish?" He ignored my jibe.

"A boatful."

"So when do you want me to show up for dinner?"

"Can I come? Can I, Jes? Can I, please?" Danny bounced up and down.

"Forget it, Shrimp. Nobody invited you."

"Nobody invited you neither."

"I don't have to be invited. I'm special. Right, Jes?" His crooked grin peeked out below the large hand covering the top half of his face.

"Yeah, yeah. You're special," I said, packing down the walls of the moat with clay so the water wouldn't seep through.

That was the thing about Sam — confidence to burn. It radiated from him like a chemical spill.

"I never get to do one thing," Danny muttered.

"You're all invited," I decided suddenly. I was cooking after all. And besides, Dad needed to socialize more. I didn't want to admit it, but it would be a relief not to have to field questions about Mom all evening. With the Schmidts there, her name wouldn't even come up.

Sam sprang to his feet in a burst of energy. "Let's take out the S.S. Minnow."

"Can I come? Can I come for a boat ride?" Danny begged.

Sam shook his head. "You'd miss out on the sand castle judging, Shrimp. You don't want to lose that ice-cream cone, do you?"

Danny's face fell. He bit his lower lip. "Nooo. Don't go, Jes. You'll get one, too, if you stay."

But Sam was already hauling me to my feet.

"We'll be back in an hour. Tell Mom, okay, Shrimp?"

Danny nodded, resigned.

"You'll win first prize, Danny Boy. I know it," I said over my shoulder.

The bright orange hull of the S.S. Minnow scraped against the pebbles as we pushed it into the water. I climbed in front; Sam took his place in the stern.

We didn't speak at first. Both of us, I think, were awed by the peacefulness. Out in the middle of the lake, it felt like nothing ever changed. We were part of something that had been here long before us and would remain long after we were gone. Something not held by time, but living nonetheless. I lay the paddle across the bow and looked down at the tiny fish nibbling at bugs just below the surface.

The canoe veered off course for a second until Sam changed his stroke to accommodate my lack of assistance.

It continued to skim across the surface of that underwater world. Tips of trees from the other side entered the reflection.

Then the canoe slowed and I heard Sam rummaging around for his camera. Gently the waves rocked us. I peered over my shoulder as I heard Sam snapping away at something only he could see.

"You must have a million pictures of that same shoreline."

He didn't answer. He was lost somewhere between the lens and whatever he was seeing. When I turned farther, I heard another click and saw the lens pointed at me.

"Not to mention a million pictures of the same me."

"You're never the same. There's always something going on."

"But how do you know when it's going to be a good picture?" I squiggled around in my seat carefully so that I was facing him.

"Well, I never know for sure until I develop it."

"Isn't that frustrating, not knowing?"

"Not really. I mean, I can usually feel it when I'm getting good stuff."

"But you can't really trust that, can you? A feeling?"

He lowered his camera so that it was dangling at his chest. He ran a hand through his shaggy hair. "What else is there?"

The question hung between us like the seagull hovering beside the boat hoping for a bread crust.

"Something more than that. Feelings change."

Sam looked vaguely disgruntled — last month's Dell word. "Sure they change ... and then they take you somewhere else. That's not a bad thing. It's like ... it's like when I look at photos I've taken a couple of years ago and I see something new. The image takes on a new meaning. A good image is always asking new questions, producing new feelings. You want things to be so certain, Jes. You want to know everything."

"What's wrong with that?"

"It's not wrong, exactly. It's ... I don't know."

"Aha!" I replied exultantly, loving to have baffled him.

He smiled and picked up his camera again. He snapped. I yelped and he smiled more broadly... the silver of his braces glinting at me from below the camera. Then he lowered it so I could see his eyes. "Where's the mystery if you know everything? Where's the fun? Besides, knowledge changes. People are always discovering stuff, pretending that it wasn't there before, but it always was. Pictures show the truth; they don't try to tell it." He was snapping shots again, and talking faster. "Telling something changes it; explaining something means you're missing something else. A picture captures everything: the beauty, the ugliness … just for the moment. It holds that moment eternally." Then he stopped, out of breath.

I swiveled back and brought the paddle over the side of the canoe. "I still want to know how things are going to turn out."

"Argh," was his final word.

I began paddling again and soon we were on the other side. The shore here was rocky and the water clear. Above us loomed the old pine tree with the swinging rope dangling from it. Frayed, heavy knots tied halfway up had been clung on to by countless kids as they swung out and dropped into the water. Sam was the undisputed king of the jumpers. I'd never done it. The rope reminded me of a hangman's noose.

"You jumping today?" he asked, as always.

"Not today," I answered, as always.

He rolled out of the boat then reached inside for his camera case. He walked to shore with it high above his head. I watched him climb the cliff path carefully but quickly, holding on to sharp rocks that jutted out. At the top, he grabbed the rope and pulled it back to the highest spot. I could see the muscles of his tanned arms bunch and strain as he lifted his body up, leaving the solid ground with one mighty push. Then he was suspended as his body hurled forward — flying — and I envied that moment all the way through me. I could actually feel it pushing against my spine. "Now," I called out. He let go of the rope and plummeted down, breaking the smooth surface with a glorious splash. I didn't know I'd stopped breathing, but I started again when I saw his head pop up beside me like a blond seal.

I knew what was next and I prepared myself for the brace of cold water. Sure enough, his paws reached up and capsized the canoe. I felt myself fall from this familiar and safe distance into the water and then I was surrounded.

"You're so predictable," I sputtered as I swam to shore.

He pushed the upside-down canoe to shallow waters and with one heave, he righted it.

"So are you."

5

Why hadn't I told Sam about Angela? I usually told him everything, sometimes even before the thoughts were fully formed.

Maybe it was because if I didn't say her name, it wouldn't be true. She wouldn't be there when I got back. It would be like one of my old nightmares and Mom coming into my room in her blue terry-cloth housecoat and stroking my hand. "Think happy thoughts, Jes. Only happy thoughts." And I'd try. I'd try so hard to push the monsters back into the shadows. But this Angela person wasn't a figment of my restless imagination.

"Should I slice the lemons or quarter them?" Dad asked over my shoulder. I jumped. He put his hand against my back and rubbed in a small circle. "Sorry, Funny Face. Didn't mean to scare you."

"It's okay. Do you think we have enough fish for everyone? Maybe we should do hot dogs for the little guys." Suddenly I was having nervous second thoughts about this dinner party.

"Good idea."

"Should I have asked before inviting them over? Sam just did his Sam thing and then, ba-boom, it all snowballed."

"Nah. This is great. I haven't seen the whole crew for a while."

A while. Our two families used to do stuff together all the time, but that had changed after the divorce. Mom and Amber were so tight — like sisters. My insides twanged the way they always did when I came up against that word. It was so long ago, but I still ... *Happy thoughts, Jes, only happy thoughts.* I shook my head free of the memory.

"Capers, Dad. Tonight I insist on capers." I mustered authority as Dad winced like a little boy being told to eat his broccoli.

"And ketchup," he said.

I whirled around still holding the bread knife, when I caught the teasing expression on his face. His hands flew above his head in a gesture of surrender.

"Just a thought," he said. "Since when did you become so passionate about cooking?"

I turned back to the crusty baguette. "I'm just trying to rise above my pedestrian station in life, Dad."

He let out a howl of laughter and the sound filled me with shock and unexpected joy. Then, just as quickly, my eyes brimmed with tears over how long it had been since I'd heard that sound.

Dad didn't seem to notice. He was still chuckling. "Pedestrian station. Good one, Jes. You sure you aren't reading my dusty books?"

I dumped the bread into a basket I'd lined with a flowered paper napkin. It wasn't linen, but I didn't think Martha Stewart would be dropping by. Just the Schmidts.

After I'd set the scarred pine table with the odd assortment of dishes we kept up here, I went outside and picked some wildflowers for the centerpiece. I arranged them in an old milk bottle and stood back to admire the effect.

"Looks great, Funny Face." Dad smiled at me. "You're growing up, aren't you?" His face wandered to someplace where I couldn't follow. I hugged him around the middle. He was losing weight, I realized. I hugged tighter to keep him with me.

"No, I'm not," I said with conviction. "I'm the same."

He just stroked my hair and we stood there until a loud knock came at the door.

Silence turned to the roar of a tidal wave as Schmidts poured into the room. Amber oohed and aahed over the table and remarked to Dad about what a lady of the house I'd become. Her voice was too jolly, forced. Geoff tried to herd the boys away from anything breakable.

"Now, if we could do something about those baggy overalls," Amber said, coming over to me and plucking one of the straps like it was the string of a banjo. "You've got such a cute little shape. I don't know why you hide it."

I felt my face redden and I grabbed the bouquet of flowers she'd brought. I looked for something resembling a vase to put them in. My body. Ugh. More changes I'd never asked for. Did a person not get to make one, single choice in their whole life? The thought made me furious. If Mother Nature or whoever it was that was in charge had cared to ask if I was interested in a new body, I'd have said, "No thank you, I'll pass. Give me extra speed, more courage, height to reach up and peer over treetops, thank you very much. Breasts and hips? I'll pass."

I grabbed an empty olive-oil tin and filled it with water. I plunked the flowers inside.

"Perfect, Jes. You've got the touch. Where should I put this cake?"

"Uh, over here. It looks delicious, Amber. Thanks. I hadn't even thought about dessert."

"Forget about dessert? I'm going to pretend I didn't hear that. It's an essential food group." She handed the cake platter to me. "Tell me, what can I do?"

I gave her a job slicing the carrots.

"Care to help me with the manly barbecuing of the fish, Geoff?" Dad asked.

Geoff followed him outside.

"Don't forget the capers," I warned.

Sam and the boys headed outside as well, but not before they'd each grabbed grubby handfuls of bread. Amber swatted Sam, the only one she could reach.

"I'm a growing boy, Ma," he protested.

"Yeah, yeah."

"Here," I called. "Give these to your dad." I threw a package of wieners at him. He caught them like a football, tucked them under his arm and flew out the door like he was going for a touchdown.

"What a noisy crew," Amber sighed, pouring herself a small glass of wine. "Want a soda, Jes? I put some in the fridge."

"I'll have one later."

There was a long silence as Amber sipped her wine and chopped carrots. I tried to think of something to talk about, but it was hard not to link Amber's being here to when Mom was still part of the deal. I could almost see Mom standing beside her, sipping wine, the two of them talking in those low, intimate tones.

"So what did you think of Angela?" Amber spoke softly.

I stopped cutting the parsley. "You knew?" I blurted out.

Amber's knife hung in the air and then she resumed chopping, looking down at the cutting board. "Me and my big mouth. Sorry, Jes. Your mother needed to run it by someone ..." Her voice trickled away.

"No problem," I lied. "I know you and Mom tell each other everything. I wasn't thinking." Each syllable matched the cutting motion of my knife.

Amber just sighed and poured herself a little more wine. Adults and their liquids. Coffee to get them going in the morning. Wine to slow them down at night.

"You know, Jes, once when I was about your age, my mother and I were in the kitchen together. I was the oldest of six, did I tell you that?" She looked over at me, but not really at me. "I must have asked her what we were having for dinner and she looked at me, real tired — I can still see her expression — she looked at me and said, 'Must you children eat every day?'"

I didn't know how to respond.

"I thought that was a remarkable thing to say. Really, the only remarkable thing I ever heard her say." Amber shook her head and continued chopping carrots.

"That was a fine meal, Jes," Geoff said, pushing himself away from the table. "Truly fine. How about a swim before we lose the sun?"

"I'll do the dishes," Amber offered.

"No, let me," Dad said, getting up with a stack of plates.

"It's okay, Steven. Go swim with the kids. But everyone clears," she added with maternal authority. Even Danny jumped up with a dish or two. There really was no question as to who was in charge of the Schmidt family.

"Great grub," Sam said as he headed to the door. "Last one to the wharf is, obviously, a loser."

"You have a slight advantage," I said.

"You mean my superior athletic ability?"

"I mean that you have a bathing suit on and I don't."

"Oh."

"Shoo. All of you." Amber herded them toward the door with a flourish of widespread arms.

Danny rushed over and gave me a quick hug. "Thanks, Jes. The hot dog was yummy." I smiled and hugged him back, following him out to the porch.

Sam was the first to the water, entering with a messy dive. Henry was a close second. Geoff did his famous belly flop, and my dad dove in with a perfect arc. Danny was last, pulling off his T-shirt as he ran down the hill toward the wharf and sending up a howl of annoyance at being last. Then, in a spray of cannonball splash that reached up and touched the pomegranate sun, he was in the water.

He was six now, wasn't he? My heart ached — another age my sister would never be.

There's no buildup to an event that changes your life forever. It's not like in the movies where people suddenly move in slow motion or the music shifts from a major to a minor key. You don't get to see the park brimming with the clatter and pull of children, the one tiny person who wanders away in the blink of a sun-filled eye, the desperate call of a name, the sound of squealing tires, the moment that shatters lives. You don't get clues.

We'd gone out for the afternoon. It was the day after my eighth birthday and we were going to spend my birthday money. We left Alberta behind with a babysitter. Mom said, "It'll just be the three of us again." I think she wanted me to feel special.

We went out for lunch and then to the toy store. It took a long time at the store because there was so much to choose from. Dad was patient. He gave me a piggyback ride even though he kept groaning that I was too big. After a while, Mom started looking at her watch and I knew I needed to decide. But it was tough — the stuffed rhinoceros or the panda — and I kept waffling back and forth. Mom's smile grew more and more forced and she stood at the end of the aisle, waiting for me. Finally Dad said, "What's it gonna be, kiddo?"

I made him hold the toys behind his back and then I chose. The rhinoceros won and I grabbed him, but at the cashier I changed my mind. By then, Mom's smile had disappeared and she groaned when I said I wanted the panda instead. I told her it was okay, it didn't matter, but it was too late. Dad had already run off to make the exchange.

When we arrived home, the police took us to the hospital. Mom and Dad went in to see her one at a time, but it was too late. She was gone. They didn't even let me see her. And while I waited outside, the only thing I could think about was if I hadn't taken so long to decide, this wouldn't have happened. I couldn't believe that one wrong choice could have such a consequence. I think I said this to my dad, that I should have picked the other toy. I only remember that he grabbed me tight and said it wasn't my fault, I should never think that. It was nobody's fault.

Sitting there in the hospital that day, I learned that life was not solid. It was flimsy ... so thread-bare in spots that you could see right through it.

When babies die — Alberta wasn't even two — they leave a perfect imprint behind, like you get sometimes with one flake of snow that lands on a window. After it's melted you can still see the outline, etched against the glass like an engraving. Alberta's imprint remained perfect, and I think what we were the most afraid of was that one day it would disappear completely.

"It's still hard, isn't it?" Amber came up behind me and put her hand on my shoulder.

The lump in my throat was too big for any words to pass.

"It'll get easier," she said.

I'd heard every version of that statement. None of them true.

"Do you want to be alone?"

I must have nodded because then I heard the screen door click. I didn't really want to be alone, but as well meaning as she was, Amber couldn't understand. And her not being able to understand made me feel even more alone. For it to get easier, we would have to forget Alberta. Forget the way she growled rather than being bothered with learning to speak, forget that annoying habit she had of pointing to everything she wanted and how we jumped to her bidding. Forget the military position she assumed in her stroller, standing on the footrest, pointing straight ahead with her right index finger. Forget that her first and only word was one I'd taught her. "Onward," she said, absolutely perfectly. She could speak if she wanted to.

Easier meant losing all of this and already it was fading. Mom and I used to talk about her a lot. Then less. But now that Mom had found Cal, even that had changed. Everything was changing.

Suddenly I remembered Angela, standing in my kitchen looking friendly and blond. She'd done nothing wrong, but the thought of her gave me a shiver.

"Goldilocks," I said to myself. Even now, as I sat out here on the porch, there was someone sleeping in my bed.

6

Dad and I didn't talk much on the drive home after the weekend, even though I was sure Amber hadn't kept quiet about what had happened. I liked her a lot, but she was a Blabbermouth with a capital B. A couple of times I thought he was about to say something, but then he stopped and mentioned the weather or how dry the forest was this summer.

He didn't like to talk about Alberta. It was like he left her memory upstairs in her room and closed the door. And then eventually he left completely.

Before the accident he was a teacher, grades five and six mostly. He was the only male teacher (never mine) in our school and the most popular, next to Ms. Nichi, who brought homemade fortune cookies to school. It always seemed like the hugest coincidence to me that just the right student would receive just the right fortune. I remember once getting, "She who talks much hears little," and I was amazed. It wasn't until I'd left the school that it occurred to me that the fortunes we received owed little to chance.

After the accident, Dad quit. At first it was a leave of absence, just for a year. But he never went back. He started making furniture out in the garage. I'd go out there with a book and watch him work, with the sound of the saw or the hammer in the background. It felt safe. Mom came out once in a while, but she'd always get around to asking him when he was going to go back to teaching. Eventually she sounded mad about it and stopped coming. I heard them arguing about it too many times. Mostly she'd accuse him of hiding, and then things would get so quiet that I couldn't hear. I thought maybe she was saying that she missed him. We both did, and I wanted things to go back to normal.

I asked him to drop me at Dell's now because I couldn't face going home just yet. I could walk from there. I kissed him good-bye and, again, he looked ready to say something, but I just waved and told him I'd see him the next weekend.

I rang Dell's doorbell, crossing my fingers in the hope that she'd be there. She had to be there. Her dad, Tim, answered.

"Hey, Jessica, how's it going? Dell's not in, but she should be back soon. Come on in." He ushered me into the house.

"Where is she?"

"Out with that good-for-nothing boyfriend of hers," he growled.

I smiled at his tone. He was a small man, only a couple of inches taller than me, but he was funny and fierce. We had that in common, I always thought.

"What do you know about this character?" he asked, heading into the kitchen. I followed, hoping he'd been baking. He always baked when he was upset or bored or didn't feel like writing, which was his job. He was a little pudgy lately, which usually meant he wasn't getting any work done.

"Not much," I answered.

"Right." He looked dubious. "Here, try one of these. New recipe."

I bit into a cookie. Delicious. "Yum. Thumbs up," I declared. "What's in it?"

"Goat cheese."

I almost gagged. I started to spit the cookie back into my hand. Tim was watching with an amused look on his face.

"Kidding."

"Funny," I said, swallowing.

"So, tell me truthfully, what's this Marshall person like?"

I sighed. "Okay. I'm not one hundred percent sure of this ... but I hear he's wanted for horse thievery."

"Horse thievery? You don't say. You don't hear much about that these days."

I shook my head. "I know! It's sad. It really is. Such an interesting crime."

Tim smiled, placing cookie dough on the sheet with his bare hands. I tried not to wonder if he'd washed them.

"Apparently he's also married," I continued, taking another cookie.

This time Tim chuckled. "Really?"

"Oh, yeah. One wife in Bonavista and the other in …"

"Let me guess? Vancouver Island?"

I grinned. "That's right. How did you know?"

"A father knows these things."

A loud crash in the hall indicated that Dell was home. Nobody would ever accuse her of being graceful.

"Hey, Jes, buddy, friend, kindred spirit —" She filled the room suddenly with her five foot, seven inch frame. (Okay, I'm jealous of that, but I'm getting over it.) "How are you? It's been forever. I have so much to tell you. Come to my room," she ordered.

"Hello, what about me? What do you have to tell me?" Tim demanded.

Dell turned and crooked her head to the side. "I have … I have … nothing to tell you." She shrugged apologetically.

"How can you have so much to tell one person and absolutely nothing for another? How can that be?" He waved his spatula like a conductor's baton.

"You're not a girl. I hate to break it to you, Dad, but you're not. Even if you do wear an apron and bake cookies." She smirked in an evil way and grabbed a couple of cookies.

He let out a grunt of disgust. "I hope you weren't expecting the Feminist of the Year award."

"Leave that for Mom," she said over her shoulder, dragging me with her. I gave Tim a sympathetic look, but I didn't resist.

She pushed me into the room ahead of her and locked the door behind us. She even pulled her desk in front of it for good measure.

"What?" I asked.

"Just taking precautions."

"For what? An invasion?"

"Exactly. My mother should be home soon and she's on the warpath."

"What have you done now?"

"Why do you assume it's my fault? Aren't you supposed to be my best friend? Maybe it's her — maybe it's her and one of her menopausal rampages."

"What have you done now?" I repeated, sitting on the beanbag chair.

She chewed her cheek, an old and, speaking personally, disgusting habit she'd had since I'd known her. "I broke curfew. Big deal. So line me up and shoot me."

"Line you up?" I laughed. "A lineup of one? That's funny."

A flash of a smile broke the scowl. "That is, I guess."

"So, how late were you?"

"One, maybe two hours."

"You're right. She is a maniac. Lock her up."

"She just makes such a big deal about stuff, you know? It's not like we were doing anything wrong. We were just talking."

"We being you and Marshall?"

"Of course, since we being you and me weren't a we last night, were we?"

"Oui."

"I don't know why she doesn't trust me. That's what I told her."

I shook my head. "She doesn't trust you because she has absolutely no reason to trust you."

Dell chewed her cheek again. "That's what she said."

"She's so onto you."

She expelled an entire mouthful of air and then some. "It's exasperating. That trust line should work. But she was such an awful teenager herself ... she hasn't forgotten a thing! She's got a memory like an elephant. And who has to pay for all her wicked years? Me. It's so unfair. You know what she actually said to me? 'Been there, done that.'"

"She's so onto you," I said again, smiling.

"I guess. So, want to hear about my date with Marshall?"

"Cal's daughter, Angela, arrived the other day," I said bluntly, knowing I'd be looking at an hour of straight Marshall if I didn't get it in now.

"Huh? Say what?" Dell sat up straight. "Cal has a daughter?"

"You knew that."

"I didn't. I did?"

I nodded. "She's going to stay with us. In my room. I have a roommate." I tried the word out as I picked up Dell's old fuzzy bear, Boots, and twisted him around in my hands.

"In your room? Holy crap, Batman." She let out a whistle. "What was your mom thinking?"

I felt a stream of pure relief rush through me. Was there anything better than somebody understanding the extremity of a situation so quickly and without explanation? I didn't think so.

But even as much as Dell understood, I still couldn't bring myself to repeat Cal's "sister" comment. Some things — even the things you most wanted to say, maybe them most of all — couldn't fit inside words, were just too big for them.

"Thinking isn't my mother's specialty these days," I shrugged. "She's in 'the zone.'"

Dell nodded, digging under the bed for her stash of chocolate. She pulled out a box. "Milk chocolate or semi-sweet?" she asked.

I shook my head.

She took one for herself, then shoved the box back. "You must be bummed. What's she like?"

"I barely even spoke to her but she's, like, perfect."

"Ugh." She took a big bite of the chocolate. "Oh well, maybe it'll be okay. Don't look so ... so ... woebegone."

"Good word," I said. "That's how I feel. Woe-begone. Be gone ... woe. Good word. How's the novel coming, by the way?" Dell had been writing a science-fiction novel since she was nine years old. It was about teenage assassins saving the world from adults. At last count it was over three hundred pages.

"I'm a little blocked," she admitted.

"You and your dad."

"Yeah. How'd you know?"

"The cookies. Dead giveaway."

"Poor guy. Last week it was cheesecake. If this keeps up, we're all going to gain ten pounds."

A loud knock came at the door, followed by a twisting of the doorknob. "Adele?" Dell's mom, Maggie, was on the other side.

"The warden," Dell whispered, getting up to move the table and unlock her door. "If I don't answer, she'll throw tear gas."

"Oh, hi, Jes," Maggie said, standing in the half-open doorway. "Your mother called. She wants you home ASAP."

"Okay, thanks. I was just leaving."

Maggie scanned the room, very much like a warden checking the cell. It really was a wonder that Dell or Mean Pammy got away with anything under that watchful eye. I could probably grow marijuana plants in my room, call them a science experiment and Mom wouldn't notice. But if I sighed more than twice — then it was therapy time. Dell and I figured our mothers were total opposites. Maggie noticed everything external; my Mom used laser techniques to drill and blast down to the molten core.

"Nice tan, Jes. You up at the lake this weekend?"

"Yup."

Her eyes narrowed. "You should be liberal with the sunscreen. You have such lovely skin."

"Mother," Dell sighed. "Could we save the mole check for later?"

Maggie sighed back. "Are you as disrespectful to your mother, Jessica?"

"Never. In fact, I was meaning to talk to Dell about it. I'm quite concerned," I said, making a face at Dell.

Maggie smiled. "You must keep this one as a friend forever, Dell. That's an order."

"Okay, if you say so." Dell stood and touched the top of the door, towering over her mom. "Just a few more minutes, okay, Warden?" Then she gently closed the door in her mother's face.

Faintly, I heard a "Grr," then footsteps in the hallway.

"You are such a big suck-up to my parents," Dell complained. "They think you're the ideal daughter."

"I like them. They're so ... straightforward, you know? No big surprises."

"Yeah, well. So, you were up at the lake? Was Sam there?"

"Listen, I gotta go. Mom will be wondering where I am."

"Don't change the subject." Dell blocked the door. "When are you going to give Sam a break?"

"I don't know what you're talking about."

She crossed her arms and leaned against the door. Serious body language. "He's wild for you."

"Wild? Oh, brother." I squirmed in my seat.

"He is," she insisted. "And getting cuter by the second ... even as we speak! You've got to move now, before those braces come off, I'm telling you."

"We're friends," I said in a small voice. "Doesn't that count for anything?"

Dell considered this. "Well, sure, it's everything with us ... but guys? They're different. Pretty soon somebody's going to snatch him up and, besides, you know he's crazy about you. He's dying to be more than friends."

"More than friends. Like being friends is so, so ... consolation prize. Do you have any idea how much I hate that?"

"Why don't you give him a chance?"

"How many people do you know who stay friends after they've broken up?"

Dell flopped down on the bed, chewing her half-eaten chocolate bar. "Jeez, Jes, you haven't even gone out with him and already you've broken up! You're a puzzle ... an enigma. Even to me."

"Good word, Dell. Gotta go."

As I walked home, I wondered how Mom knew I was already back from the lake. Then I realized I'd left my stuff in Dad's car. He probably dropped it off on the way home, which meant he'd likely met Angela. And was wondering why I hadn't said anything.

I kicked a stone across the road and watched it skitter to the curb. Everything was getting more confusing and more complicated. And I was starting to feel like Alice in Wonderland — getting smaller and smaller.

7

For some bizarre reason, I almost knocked at my own front door. It had only been a couple of days, but I knew something had changed, shifted.

Plate tectonics. We'd learned about it in school. Every land mass on a different plate, shifting at an almost imperceptible pace ... no perceivable movement, yet responsible for mountains and volcanoes and earthquakes. And while I was gone, I knew this house had shifted. None of the neighbors would know, but I could feel it. Edging toward something — a volcano, an earthquake? That part I didn't know.

When I walked in, she was sitting on a couch in the living room with her feet up and a magazine in her hand.

The feet dropped to the carpet when she saw me and she stood up. I wished she hadn't. She was so tall. Basketball scouts everywhere would have drooled at the sight. Five foot ten, at least. She'd pulled her long hair up into a ponytail, but bits of it were drooping and twirling *fetchingly* (last week's Dell-word) around her chin and she had a faint sheen of sweat on her face. It was a hot day, after all. But on her it looked applied ... intentional. Dabbed on by a photographer. Perfect.

"Hi, Jes. I was waiting for you. Your mom's in the kitchen. She said you'd be home soon."

"Well, here I am. Home soon. That's me. I'm home." I was babbling and I knew it. "Soon."

She smiled, just a little. "It's nice to see you again. It was kind of quick the other day. Your mom said you had to go to your father's place, so that was why you rushed off."

"Yup."

"Did you have a nice time at the lake?"

"Yeah, my dad got the ... well, he has a cabin. We spend a lot of time up there in summer." So you won't be seeing much of me, I added to myself.

"He said."

"Huh?"

"Your dad. When he dropped off your stuff. He seems really nice. He invited me to come up with you some time."

My heart did a triple flip before settling in the pit of my stomach.

"This is going to be fun, don't you think, Jes? It's Jes, right? Or do you prefer Jessica? You can call me Angela or Angel — some of my friends call me Angel, but only if they don't know me very well, ha ha. Just kidding."

I forced my cheek muscles to pull the corners of

my mouth into a smile. "Jes is fine," I said. "I'm just going to go put my stuff away." I edged toward the door, but she followed.

"I'll help you."

"It's okay," I started to protest, but she showed no sign of turning back.

It was just as well that she was with me when I entered my room because otherwise I might have screamed.

The room had been cleaned.

Except *cleaned* wasn't the word for it. The room had been sterilized. You could have performed surgery on the floor and not thought twice about infection. This was not the normal state of my room. Usually there was a comfortable balance between mess and living space. Mom called it a refugee camp; I thought of it as an ecosystem ... a delicate ecosystem with everything doing its job, proclaiming that I was there — that I *was*. But this room ... this place screamed out, "Vacancy."

"You like?" Angela or Angel or whoever she was looked directly at me. Or as directly as she could, considering the extra height she had on me.

"It's, uh, really tidy."

"Yeah, well. Elli and I worked hard yesterday. Your mom said you used to train elephants in here. She's really funny, your mom. I like her a lot. So does my dad. Well, duh. Ha ha. They're getting married. But I think it's great. I mean, obviously divorce sucks, but, well, if at first you don't succeed, try, try again, right? That's my motto. And besides, it's not like my mother hasn't had a gazillion boyfriends. So, how about you?"

"How about me — what?" My head was spinning. Did this girl have a string attached to her back that pulled out and made her chatter like that doll I had when I was six years old?

"How about you, do you have a motto? How about you, are you in favor of this marriage or, how about you, do you like the room? Take your pick. Answer on whatever level you'd like."

Oh, crap. She was smart, too.

"You can never be too clean. That's my motto." I said, unzipping my knapsack.

"Right, okay. Well, I'll go downstairs and see if Elli needs help with dinner."

I put my clothes away and wondered if I had just won this round or lost? Not knowing made me think I'd probably lost.

"Good dinner, Elli," Angela gooed appreciatively at my mother. "The best so far." She had well-honed sucking-up skills, that was for sure.

Cal leaned back on his chair, hands linked behind his head. He looked satisfied "It was delicious, El. What was in that sauce?"

Mom just smiled. I could have told him it was cream of mushroom soup, but I didn't. I figured he should have a few surprises in store for him after the big day.

"I'll do dishes," Angela jumped up from her chair.

"It's okay, Angela. I'm pretty sure Jes is going to volunteer. She's probably just waiting for the right moment."

"Oh, right. I was, I was. I wanted it to be special, but no time like the present, right? So, how about I do the dishes?"

"That would be lovely, dear. I'm going to show Angela the photo albums."

"Ooh, lucky Angela," I said under my breath.

"Here, I'll help you, Jes. It's the least I can do," Cal offered.

Boy, you said a whole mouthful there, I thought, taking a stack of dirty dishes into the kitchen. Without Cal, would any of this be happening? Okay, maybe the divorce wasn't his fault, but then again, if he hadn't showed up, who knew? You heard about remarriages all the time. All the time. It was practically a cliché.

"It's okay, Cal. I can load the dishwasher."

"Scrape and rinse. Isn't that the order of the day?"

"The order of my mother, you mean."

"Same thing."

"You catch on fast," I said without thinking.

But Cal only smiled. As if he knew.

It only took us five minutes to get the kitchen in

order. My mother has this way of cleaning up as she goes … kind of like a cat.

"You mind helping me outside, Jes?" Cal asked. "I'm going to take some of those plums off your mom's hands. The tree's loaded with them."

Outside, the last of the evening sun was sinking in the west — somewhere. In town, it was difficult to tell exactly where the sun made its final dip. At the lake it was different. The sun was there one second and then it wasn't, slipping silently behind the mountain.

"Aren't these beauties?" Cal said, holding a ripe plum in his hand.

"I guess." This plum tree had been giving us its fruit as long as I could remember.

He placed it in a basket carefully and I plucked a few from the lower branches. The treetop reached over Sam's backyard and I wondered if they'd returned from the lake yet.

"Have you seen a more beautiful color?" Cal held out a plum for me to inspect. "I mean, even with that thin layer of dust, or maybe because of it — the deep purple against the leaves. It's gorgeous, don't you think?"

"Sure," I answered, picking plums. This was the kind of conversation Mom liked to have. "Sure" usually did the trick.

"I was just thinking that sometimes a person has this heightened awareness of how beautiful things are, and you realize how much you must miss during regular life."

"Okay."

"I sound nuts, huh?" He grinned at me between two leafy branches.

"Sorta," I admitted.

We continued picking in silence. There was only so much a person could say about plums. "Gee, they're a nice shape, aren't they?" Right. He was a nice guy. Dell was right about that. But you don't have to go out and marry a guy just because he's nice. I honestly figured he was a stage my mom was going through. Some mid-life thing. When she told me they were getting married, I'd been stunned.

"You hardly even know him!" I'd said.

Then I'd had to listen to a whole new speech about moving forward and getting on with life and ... who knows ... the importance of not wearing white shoes after Labour Day. I had stopped listening.

"Whatever," I'd finally muttered and Mom had looked hurt, so I tried to look happy for her.

I looked at Cal now through the leaves and tried to imagine him in our house every morning and every night. He grinned at me again. I dropped a plum and bent to pick it up to avoid returning the grin. There was far too much grinning going on around here these days. When I straightened, his face was back to normal, except that he looked even more earnest than usual.

"The other day, Jes. The comment I made about you having a new sister? That was really insensitive. I guess I was a little nervous ... I didn't think. I'm sorry."

I backed away from the tree toward the house. "It's okay. I have some stuff to do, okay, Cal?"

"Sure. Thanks for helping."

I moved quickly into the house and up the stairs. At the top, I felt shaky. I had figured my mother would tell him about Alberta. But ... they had talked about her. He thought he knew about her. He wasn't just moving into this house. He was moving into our lives.

I went to my room, hoping to avoid human contact, but when I opened the door, there was Angela — sitting on her bed (previously known as my horizontal closet).

"I thought you were looking at photo albums," I said.

"Your mom got a phone call. One of her clients, I think. She had that look on her face."

"That look?" She knew my mother's looks already?

"Yeah. Like my dad gets. The I'm-ready-to-save-the-world look. They're sure alike, aren't they?"

"I don't know," I shrugged, mad that she'd made the same observation I had.

"So how bummed are you exactly that I'm here?"

"I'm not bummed," I lied.

"Okay, whatever. Your call." She went back to flipping through her magazine.

"I mean, he's your dad," I said, feeling the need to add evidence to my lie. "You should be at his wedding, right?"

"Ah, yes, dear Watson. True enough. But the wedding's not for four weeks. 'Why on earth is she here already?' Isn't that what you're really thinking?" She said all this without even looking up from her magazine.

"Check this one out," Angela held up the magazine, showing a beautiful girl in a skimpy bikini. "Hundred bucks says she's bulimic," she muttered, lowering it and inspecting the picture like it was a slide under a microscope.

"I don't usually put money on eating disorders," I answered, thinking that Angela's body didn't look a whole lot different than the model's. Suddenly I was glad to have my baggy overalls on.

"Nobody has a waist that small," she was saying under her breath.

"I think I'll go take a shower," I said suddenly. At least I'd be alone there. I stopped at the door. "So then, why did you come ... a month early?" I blurted out.

Angela's bright-green eyes looked up at me. "My mom kicked me out. She's in the middle of a crisis. Personally, I think she's threatened by me ... you know, I'm a reminder of her fading beauty, days gone by … roads not taken? That sort of thing. Classic, really."

"She kicked you out?" I was still back on that one.

"Well, not exactly," she shrugged. "She said, 'If you're not happy here, you can always live with your father.' So I went up to my room, packed my stuff, called the bus station and here I am!"

"Just like that?"

"Sure. I'm a free spirit, Jes," she smiled, and the dimples in her face creased prettily. "I like that name. It's nice. Listen, I believe in taking control of your own destiny … doing what you want … standing at the top of the mountain and screaming out, 'I'm here!'"

"Huh." This was my brilliant response.

"You know what else?"

I shook my head.

"You're very cute. I always wanted to be short. I never have been, always was the tallest in my class. Yuck. Except it's good for modeling, which is what I'm going to be, as well as an actress … and maybe, who knows? Maybe I'll discover something … the Lost City of Atlantis or a really excellent breast implant that doesn't leak. I could use some help in that area." She looked down at her chest, which, as far as I could discern, seemed to be doing just fine. "Anyway, where was I? Oh, yeah, your cuteness." She walked over to the bureau and pulled open the top drawer. "This is too small for me, but it will look fabulous on you. Try it on," she ordered.

I caught the garment midair. It was a T-shirt encrusted with the slogan "psycho" in sparkly sequins. It still had the price tag on it.

"It's sort of expensive … I shouldn't," I protested, wondering where I would ever wear such a shirt.

"C'mon. It's a — gesture of goodwill. We're going to be sisters, you know."

I nodded dumbly. "I'm … just going to take that shower."

"Hey!" she almost shouted. "Your motto!"

"What?"

"You can never be too clean!" She grinned her father's grin.

"Huh," I said, clutching the shirt as I left the room and walked across the hall to the bathroom. I closed the door and locked it behind me. Angela's makeup had been placed neatly on a shelf in the medicine cabinet. A blow drier, curling iron and some other device that looked like it might be useful for implementing torture were lined up on the counter.

When I stepped into the shower, I noticed that even the grout scum had been scrubbed away. As I stood beneath the hot water, I had a really clear picture in my head of Angela standing on a mountain or maybe on the roof of our house shouting, "I'm here!" I could totally see it.

8

Mom had cut back her hours at the center to concentrate on wedding plans and this was right up Angela's alley, if you could trust the sounds of delight she emitted as they sat with heads bent over bridal magazines. Neither one of them had any trouble, it seemed, with the fact that it was the second go-round and that they were planning a celebration, the major theme of which was "till death do us part." Considering that my dad and Angela's mom were still very much alive, this seemed a considerable oversight to me.

Anyway, it looked like they had everything under control and I made to duck out the back door and shoot some baskets.

"Aren't you coming to the caterer with us?" Mom asked, not even looking up from the table.

"Kennedys', Mom," I answered, using my baby-sitting job as an excuse.

"On Thursdays? I thought you got Thursdays off."

"She needs a pedicure or something."

"She can take Lucy with her," she said. "It wouldn't kill her to spend some time with her daughter."

"Is that a professional opinion, Mom?" I asked, only half joking. I really worried about Lucy, too.

"I wouldn't turn her away if she wanted therapy," Mom answered. "Oh well, none of my business, right?" she added. "Anyway, that's not until this afternoon. Come with us."

"Yeah, Jes. It'll be fun," Angela cooed.

Mom threw an extra look my way. "There will be food."

Ten minutes later, Angela was filling the car with questions about the wedding and managing to sidestep every query my mother volleyed back about her life in California. It was an interesting exchange and almost made up for the fact that I was going to spend a beautiful summer morning tasting cardboard sandwiches and whipped topping. But by the time we'd reached our destination, I was filled with a grudging respect for Angela's ability to talk a lot without really saying anything. Had my mother met her match?

The caterer turned out to be a homemade-cookie grandma type.

"I could live with this," I said as I sniffed the fragrant air that drifted from the house when she opened the front door. My kind of perfume:

cinnamon, vanilla ... possibly chocolate. In the kitchen I saw a pan of freshly baked croissants.

"Have one, please," Mrs. Sara Lee invited.

"Yes, please." I lunged for the counter and took one. It was still warm, sagging wonderfully in the middle with the weight of gooey chocolate.

Both Angela and my mother passed, but I was too overtaken with awe over the delicate balance of flavors — butter, almond paste, deep rich chocolate — to care. "You're hired," I said with my mouth full.

I happily occupied myself with finishing the croissant as Mom and Angela peppered the lady (Mrs. Cameron, it turned out) with questions.

It seemed that Angela was in favor of caviar and flowing champagne, while my mother was inclined toward simpler fare. Another interesting interchange ensued and I was starting to see how similar they were — both being polite, but neither willing to back down. I wasn't sure who I'd put my money on. Mom had age and experience on her side, but Angela had a boatful of youthful determination. Mrs. Cameron gave me a glass of milk and I decided to enjoy the spectacle, watching a couple of gladiators circling each other. When Mrs. Cameron offered another croissant, I didn't turn it down, even when Angela whispered how they were absolutely brimming with saturated fat. I thanked her for the information, but my sarcasm was lost on her as Mom was, at that moment, suggesting salmon.

"Only one entrée?" Angela looked aghast.

Mom turned to her with almost perfect posture. Knew that one. It was the in-another-life-I-was-a-queen stance. I licked the last of the chocolate from my fingers as they finally agreed on a menu. Salmon and goat cheese. It occurred to me that my opinion was not asked once.

"What? No piggies-in-a-blanket?" I said, just for fun.

They looked equally shocked and I mentally noted another similarity: zero sense of humor.

"Kidding," I offered, weakly.

"Another croissant?" Mrs. Cameron asked, and I was tempted to say yes, just to see their eyes bulge out, but my belly was already stretched to capacity. I actually felt a little sick, so I said no thanks and contented myself with the joint relief on their faces.

"Jes, Jes, Jes." Lucy flung open the door and threw herself in my arms. "You're here."

"Lucy, Lucy, Lucy," I answered, hugging her back. "So are you."

"Don't climb all over her. Jessica isn't the monkey bars at the park." Mrs. Kennedy approached the entrance with the click clack of high heels on hardwood. As often as she wore heels, she still looked as though she might topple over with a good gust of wind.

I liked Lucy a lot. But Mrs. K was something else. She called Lucy "the girl" when she talked about her. Mostly she seemed to ignore her. Lucy seemed to be an inconvenience, especially in the summertime when school was out. There was no talk of a Mr. Kennedy, so I figured there was some sad story in that department.

"It's okay, Mrs. Kennedy. I'm climbable today," I said, pointing to the side pockets of my cargo pants. "Perfect for scaling."

Lucy scrambled up and I held her in my arms. Part of me was saying, "See, this is how it's done," but I didn't think Mrs. K would catch on.

Sure enough, she looked down her powdered nose, bemused. "Well, then. There's lunch for you and the girl in the refrigerator. I'll be home by four o'clock." She left her scent hovering in the air behind her.

Lucy waved until her mother was gone, even though Mrs. K walked straight to the car without a backward glance. The wistful look in the little girl's eyes made my own prickle.

"Okay, Lucy-Goosie, time for checkers. I feel like jumping all your kings today."

"No way," she shouted, scrambling down from my arms. "No possible way."

I knew she was right. Lucy played "creative

checkers," which meant she got to change the rules whenever she wanted. If she was in a jam, she'd move sideways, backward, diagonally — whatever it took. Rules made little impression on Lucy. The name of the game was to survive with as many pieces left on the board as possible. I just hoped she could keep it up for the rest of her childhood. It might help her survive her mother.

There were two messages on the machine when I got home. The first was from Dad saying he'd pick me up at noon tomorrow. Yay, I thought. Old times. Or at least the closest I could get. The second was from Dell, and she was using her Imperial Princess voice.

"I've not heard from you since Sunday. If you're not dead, and part of you better be, call me ASAP."

I punched speed dial four. Dell answered after one ring.

"Which part of me better be dead?" I asked, without even a hello.

"The part of you that's responsible for keeping in touch with your best friend."

I didn't bother saying that in this great summer of Marshall, she'd been pretty dismal in that department herself.

"So how come you haven't invited me over to meet the goddess?"

"She and my mother are too busy planning the royal wedding. Besides, you know I baby-sit during the day."

"Still, there's the nights, although I have been pretty busy with Marshall." Her voice softened like cardboard left in the rain at the mention of his name.

"How is the old sheriff doing?"

"He's great. He's so intense. We have such great … intense times together. Did I tell you he writes poetry?"

"*Great, intense* poetry?" I guessed.

"Yeah, really," she said, totally serious. She hadn't even caught my tone.

"You know, Jes." Her voice shifted. "If you would just cut Sam some slack, we could go on a double date or something."

I made a soft, clicking sound on the telephone with my fingernail, hoping it would sound like call waiting.

"Hold on, Dell. There's another call —" I started to push the mute button.

"Okay, okay. Consider the subject changed," she said.

"Thank you."

"So is it too weird — having her there?"

"Imagine Mean Pammy in your bedroom 24/7."

I heard Dell's gasp of horror. Then, "Why doesn't she just use the other — you know."

Alberta's bedroom. It made sense, really. But only in the real world ... out there. In here, that room was already occupied. I couldn't think of anything to say and the air between us lengthened.

"Dumb idea ... Sorry, Jes," Dell faltered.

"It's okay. Anyway, it's kind of a relief because now I don't have to worry about jumping up and down with excitement over wedding plans, you know?"

"Like you were."

"I jumped," I defended myself, "occasionally. Anyway, it's good to have some of the pressure off. I swear if I had to look at one more periwinkle fabric swatch ..."

"Oh, Jes, I've seen the pattern. The dress is going to be gorgeous. On you," she added, almost as an afterthought.

"I'm going to look ridiculous."

"You're petite —"

"Dell, call waiting. Gotta go."

"Okay, okay, liar. I've got to phone Marsh anyway. So, you're up at the lake this weekend?"

"Yup."

"I'm going to try to talk Dad into bringing the boat up. I'll come by if we go."

"Good. I hope you do," I said sincerely. "One, two, three ..." And then we hung up.

As I put the phone down, Mom's car pulled up in the driveway. She and Angela walked up the front stairs laden with bags and packages, voices bright and brimming.

It took me a second to get used to Mom's appearance. Instead of her usual style — business or business casual — she was wearing jeans, and they were flared at the bottom. Her T-shirt had embroidery on it and a cardigan was tied around her hips. She looked as though she'd fallen headfirst into The Gap.

She blushed as she caught my gaze. "Too young? It was Angela's idea."

I shook my head, dumbfounded. Angela was now dressing my mother?

"You look terrific," Angela insisted with obvious fashion authority.

"Oh, Jes, you should see what we found. The most gorgeous material —"

She pulled out a filmy length of silky, bluey-purple fabric and spread it across my shoulder. It floated down to the ground.

"Togas? Inspired, Mom. You'll make Wedding of the Year for sure."

Mom smiled. "I knew it would bring out the color of your eyes. Angela thought it would, too. You girls are going to look just lovely."

"Girls?" I said.

Mom looked at me and I could see the "oops" in her eyes.

"Didn't I tell you? I've asked Angela to be a bridesmaid."

I felt a phony smile place itself on my mouth without asking permission. Angela's expression was giving nothing away.

"You didn't mention that, no," I managed to say.

"Won't it be fun? I always wanted to be in a wedding party when I was young," Mom said oddly, like this had anything to do with anything.

"If it's not okay with you, Jes, I'll understand," Angela said clearly, and I admired her bluntness. Admired it and hated it, too.

"No, it's fine. Like Mom says, it'll be fun," I punctuated the word "fun" with an even phonier smile.

But Mom just gave me a quick hug. She'd chosen to believe me. Then she packed up the fabric carefully in the tissue paper. "It'll be wonderful," she said quietly. She looked tired.

"Your mom's really pumped about the wedding, huh?" Angela asked later as she and I did the supper dishes. Mom and Cal had gone for a walk.

"Uh-huh," I mumbled, clanging and rattling cutlery.

"My Dad's pretty excited, too. I haven't spent much time with him — just a few summers — but I've never seen him so happy."

"Yeah, well." I slid the last dish onto the plastic rack and closed the door, clicking the machine on. It rumbled into action with its traditional roar.

"Horrible machine," I said. "I'm going outside."

From the porch I took a long shot at the basketball hoop. It hit the rim but went in through the net.

"Nice shot," Angela said, coming up behind me. She walked over to retrieve the ball. I remembered the summer that Dad put the pad in. He'd wanted it to be cement, but Mom preferred paving stones because they looked better. So he'd spent weeks digging up the hard-packed clay ground, smoothing it out and putting the pavers in — red and gray — so that it looked really nice. It still looked as good as the summer he'd done it.

I snapped out of the memory as I saw Angela sink a perfect shot. She lined up and shot another. And another. Four balls in succession swooshed through the net. Her form was nearly perfect. I felt a worm of jealousy wedge its way into my gut.

"Nice," I called out.

Angela brushed a crinkly strand of hair away from her face. "Thanks. I play some, but I'm a little rusty."

Rusty? If that was rusty, give me a little, please.

"Want to play one on one?" she asked.

"Not right now," I said, leaning back in the lounge chair.

Angela played a while longer, with her long hair fluttering behind like an unfurled flag. She was more than good; she was at home on the court. And the more I watched her, the more the little worm inside me wriggled and grew.

Finally she tired and, with a faint skiff of sweat on her face, she sat on the wicker chair opposite me.

"So, have you thought about a wedding present?" she asked.

"No, not really. Have you?"

Angela tilted her head back. "I'm torn between dishes — Elli showed me the ones they want — or maybe some pottery. It's really ..."

I drifted off as Angela did a catalogue count-down of possible wedding gifts. One time when Mom and I were having one of our "let's really talk" talks about the divorce and my feelings, she had described marriage as a slot machine, one of her many "word pictures."

"It's like you can put in quarter after quarter and keep pulling the lever, but eventually you realize you're never going to hit the jackpot. So you have to walk away — especially when you've used your last quarter."

"So, what do you think, Jes? Any of those sound good to you?" Angela's voice poked through my thoughts.

"I think I'm going to give them a roll of quarters."

Two faint lines of confusion emerged on Angela's perfect forehead. But it was my mother's appearance in the doorway that caught my attention. She'd heard my comment and knew exactly what I was talking about.

"You're never going to forgive me, are you?" she said quietly. Then she turned and walked back into the house.

9

I should've talked to Mom about what happened, should've said that I was feeling bummed about Angela's expert basketball shots, or maybe that I was grouchy or had PMS. I should've said anything to make it right between us, except the truth. I couldn't tell her she was right.

"You're pretty quiet, Jes. Everything okay?" Dad asked now.

He'd picked me up right on time and as we sped away from the city, I tried to put the last few days out of my mind.

"I'm fine."

"How's it going with, uh, Cal's daughter?"

He always paused before saying Cal's name. Always.

"She seems really nice," he continued, not waiting for an answer. "You know, if you wanted to invite her to the lake sometime, that would be okay. It might be nice for you ... having a —"

I stopped breathing for a second and looked out the window, concentrating on counting the telephone poles as they sped by. One, two, three …

He turned on the radio and we listened to classical music.

I watched the scenery pass the window … the increasing greenness, even though the lake was only an hour away from town. The thickening of blue cornflowers in the ditch was the sign that we were almost there. When I was little, I'd holler "Mara" as soon as I noticed. Now I just noticed.

I helped bring the groceries to the cabin.

"I wonder if Leonard is back," Dad mused as he put pasta and a bottle of marinara sauce in the fridge.

"I'll go check," I volunteered quickly, heading out the door.

"See if he wants to go fishing," Dad called after me.

I grabbed the rusty bike out of the shed and hopped on. Sam called it "Rusty," of course. I just called it the rusty bike. The path to Leonard's cabin was a little overgrown, and I had to be careful to avoid the gnarled roots that had sent me sprawling more than once.

Leonard always took off during July, saying he was too cranky to cope with the motorboats and Sea Doos that invaded his beloved lake during the busiest summer month. Ordinarily he was funny and easygoing, but something about the grinding, endless drone of engines wound him like a mousetrap ready to spring.

Leonard was as much a part of the lake as the big pine tree that held the rope swing, the wharf we dove off of and the moss that grew thick on the roof of his ramshackle, fairy tale cabin. It was a place where pigs and wolves and wandering children might find themselves together. Leonard never seemed a part of real life. Sometimes I even wondered which came first, Leonard or the lake.

Once, he talked about his childhood, and it was the only time I saw him distressed. His father had a fondness for drink, he said. His brothers and sisters left home as soon as they were able, leaving him — the youngest — behind. And then his mother left. He didn't say much about this, only that he had stayed with his father until he couldn't anymore. It wasn't that he didn't want to stay, it was that he couldn't.

I hadn't known how to respond. The thought of leaving a parent was inconceivable to me. But I had reached for his hand and held it.

As I approached the cabin with its sagging, mossy roof, I felt a weight slip from my shoulders. Flinging the bike to one side of the path, I rang the cowbell that hung by the side of the front door.

There was no answer at first, so I pulled again, desperately wanting him to be there.

"You're back," came a voice behind me.

I smiled before I even looked. He was always as quiet as a cat.

"*You're* back," I corrected him.

"We're both back," he compromised, patting me on the head like he always did.

Leonard wasn't the cozy, huggy grandpa type. And he wasn't the distant, cool mountain-man type either. Leonard was ... well, he just was.

"Tea?" he offered.

I nodded and followed him into the cabin. The air smelled musty, which told me he hadn't been back for long. The small room was filled with mementos of the travels he took when he wasn't at the lake.

Carved animals from Africa, tapestries and rugs from the Far East, books written in foreign languages. I picked out what I thought to be a new one and ran my fingers over the spine. I didn't recognize the language.

"Where's this from?" I asked.

"Turkey."

"Cool. What was that like? Spend any time in Turkish prisons? I've heard they're the worst."

Leonard smiled just a little, handing me a cup of tea. "I see you're as cheeky as ever. How's Sam doing, speaking of cheeky? Still taking pictures of everything in sight?"

"Pretty much. He's fine. I'm surprised he hasn't been up here to see you yet. Dad says hi ... wants to know if you want to go fishing." As I talked I wandered around, filling my eyes with the familiar sight of all Leonard's wonderful things. This place was magical to me. I spotted something new in the corner, and as I approached it, I realized it had eyes and I jumped back, startled.

"What's that?" I asked, pointing.

"Oh, that's Bliss."

"Bliss? Is she ..."

"Dead as a doornail," Leonard shrugged. "Died saving my friend's life, so he had her stuffed."

I walked over to the dead hero and ran my fingers over the ... the ... "I didn't know pigs were hairy."

"She's a Vietnamese pot-bellied pig."

"What happened to her?"

"There was a fire and she warned my friend. She died of smoke inhalation."

"She's so small."

Leonard nodded, taking a sip of tea. "She was young." He closed his eyes. "Can't you feel the breeze of the Mediterranean when you taste that?"

"Why did your friend give you, er, Bliss?"

Leonard opened his eyes about halfway and the lines around them crinkled in a smile that was mostly hidden by his teacup. "You ask a lot of questions, child. Drink your tea."

I took a cautious sip. Leonard wasn't known for brewing weak tea. "Good," I decided.

"Magnificent," he corrected. "Don't be afraid to be knocked off your chair, young lady. Try it again. This time close your eyes."

I did as I was told and took a longer sip. This time I let the tea and all its flavors travel along the side of my mouth to the back of my tongue. The pungent taste, almost spicy, burst in my mouth, waking up every sleeping taste bud. "Okay, magnificent," I agreed.

Leonard nodded. "So then, what's going on with you?"

I hesitated for only a moment, but the tea, or the cabin, or Leonard had worked its magic and I began to talk.

"Mom's getting married — remarried — in less than a month. Cal's daughter, Angela, is living with us now and Mom asked her to be a bridesmaid and she's, like, beautiful."

"So are you," he interrupted, but I ignored this.

"Dad's in a total fog about the whole thing, but it's not like he'll actually *do* anything about it. And it feels like it's all up to me."

All of these words tumbled unbidden out of my mouth. "It's like one of those Christmas bobbles where the snow confetti floats around in the water if you shake it up? It's like there's this big hand wrapped around my world and every time the debris starts to actually settle down, ba-boom, the hand just shakes it all up again." I shook my head.

"Everything's just turning bad, like old potato salad. Basically, my life sucks."

Leonard watched me carefully, still holding the mug in his hands. His hands were the most unusual thing about him. His face was practically unlined, and his hair, which he wore in a ponytail, was still mostly dark. But his hands looked as though they'd lived forever.

"So." He stood and took my cup and his own to the sink. He pulled the curtains open and a wedge of sunlight illuminated the scratched wooden floor. "Time to fish?"

I got up and as I passed the little pig, I gave it a pat on the snout. "Such a short life," I said.

"Short but infinitely wide," he said, holding the door open for me.

I walked the rusty bike along the path beside Leonard. He towered above, and I had to lean back in order to look into his eyes, but I didn't mind because it was the same way you'd look to see a bird in a tree or a star in the night sky. I liked the way Leonard never tried to solve things. I liked the way he listened to me. I especially liked the way he said things, even when I didn't understand them.

Dad was happy to see Leonard. I thought maybe he was even relieved to have company in the boat after our awkward car conversation. Or maybe it was only my relief.

Just as we were about to push off from the wharf, Sam came running up the beach, hair askew from sleep and his camera banging against his chest. He was holding his fishing rod.

Dad and Leonard laughed as he slid to a halt on the wharf, coming close to flying headlong into the water.

"Any room for me?" He gasped for air, trying suddenly and unsuccessfully to look nonchalant.

"Scoot over, Jes," Dad instructed.

I moved over and held on to the side while Sam galumphed his way into the boat.

"Why do I always have to be squished?" I grumbled, even though I was happy to have him along.

"Because you're the littlest elf," Sam said, and I was sorry I'd asked.

Once we'd made it out to a quiet nook and put our lines into the water, I felt the problems that seemed so terrible earlier begin to drift away. Things were smooth out here at least. Smooth and sane and the same.

Sam intermittently fished and took pictures and filled the air with chatter.

"It's like fishing with a squirrel," I said.

Sam grabbed my shoulders and pretended to turf me over the side of the boat, which he could have actually done if he was serious.

"Leave me alone, squirrel-man," I warned. I saw

Dad and Leonard exchange an amused look, and I shook Sam off.

We didn't catch any fish, but we ate sandwiches and laughed and Leonard told his stories of the last month.

We decided to head back at four o'clock.

"Jes'll be needing her Slurpee fix, isn't that right?" Dad teased.

"I wouldn't turn one down." I shrugged.

"Sounds good to me," Sam backed me up, holding his camera up for another picture.

I put my hands over my face, but Sam snapped anyway.

"What do you do with all those pictures?" Dad asked.

Sam just shrugged. Once, he told me that his pictures were how he made sense of life — one frame at a time.

"I have some film I'd like you to develop for me, if you don't mind, Sam," Leonard said.

Sam nodded. "Sure thing. More black and white?"

"Yes."

"Good."

Dad had been quieter than usual, and now, as he packed up the poles and gear, he looked light-years away. Sam silently and fluidly took a picture of his profile and suddenly I saw what Sam was seeing: someone lost and alone even in a boatful of people.

Heading into shore, we were quieter than on the trip out. Still, it had been a good day. My skin was warm and tight from the sun. I stood on the wharf tying up the boat when the roar of a motor interrupted the stillness.

"Jes, Jes, there you are."

"Here I am," I said, before turning to see who it was.

I recognized Tim right away in the wild Hawaiian shirt that embarrassed his daughter to the "depths of her being." Beside him in the front seat was Marshall, his mouth turned up only slightly at the corners so as not to destroy the image of the tortured soul that he was. I expected to see Dell and there she was, in a bright-red one piece.

I didn't expect to see the girl beside her. She was wearing board shorts and a tiny little T-shirt that showed her perfectly flat stomach. Her hair flowed around her shoulders in a mass of shiny waves.

Angela.

10

Sam was obviously not expecting her either. Maybe if he had been he would have tried a little harder to avoid having his jaw dip somewhere around the middle of his chest.

Tim backed the motorboat to the wharf. The bubbles and fumes from the motor left a slick on the water, and I could see Leonard wincing. Dell and Angela grinned at me from behind dark glasses.

"C'mon. We're going to the rope swing. You have your suit on, don't you? Sam, this is Angela ... Angela, this is Sam." Dell's words tripped over each other.

"How did, when did ..." I looked back at Dell, then to Angela, wishing they'd take off their stupid glasses so I could see something other than toothpaste smiles.

"My mom was telling your mom that we were going up to the lake and your mom had to go in to work, so she thought ..."

I held up my hand. Dell was over-explaining, which meant she knew this was a code blue: "I know this sucks, but what could I do?"

"I should help Dad unload the boat and clean the, er —" I remembered too late that we'd been skunked in the fish department.

"It's okay, kiddo. You go have fun with your friends."

Leonard had already headed toward the shore, my only ally. He was always shy around Dell, like he didn't quite know what to make of her. Sam had jumped into the boat, not needing a second invitation, and was chatting with Marshall while casting sidelong glances at Angela.

"Come, Jes ... don't be a poop," Dell said.

"It's pretty full in there."

"Always room for you," Tim bellowed, captainlike. "Hop in."

Against my better judgment, I stepped into the boat and sat between Angela and Dell, murmuring a hello to Angela. Her smile was still in place, but her mirrored sunglasses reflected only my own small face. I felt like a mouse in a cornfield. Even sitting, everyone loomed above me.

Tim revved the motor and, with a lurch, we sped away from the wharf. Within seconds, Dad's waving figure disappeared.

It was hard to carry on a conversation over the noise, but I was glad to have a chance to collect my thoughts. My fear had come true: worlds were colliding. Why had I thought this place would be safe, excluded from the reality of a shifting universe? Everything changed.

As we neared the rope swing, the boat slowed, then came to a stop. The boys and Dell jumped out and helped Tim moor the boat on the sandy part of the shore. After we'd clambered out, he gave us the familiar warning, "Now means now." Then he wandered off to his favorite cove to smoke the cigar he thought none of us knew about.

"Now means now." I'd heard that since we'd started coming to the rope swing. Then the jumping was supervised by parents. The rule was that when Tim or my dad yelled, "Now," you jumped. No questions, no hesitation, no nothing, or you'd end up spiraling back toward the jagged cliff. I'd watched countless others grab that knotted rope, pull their bodies up and go winging out in midair where, at the collective, "Now," they'd plummet into the water.

When we came here after my parents split for good, I knew as soon as I saw the dangling rope that I'd never do it. Letting go in any form was a type of death.

Sam and Dell were the first to shimmy up the path now. Marshall followed, then Angela and me.

"You don't have to do it," I said to Angela.

Angela nodded.

I heard Dell shout, "Now," and then saw Sam's form flying through the air, landing in a straight line with a minimal splash.

"Show off," I muttered.

"Pardon?" Angela asked, but she was looking directly at Sam as he swam to the shore below us.

"Nothing."

"So what's the deal with this Sam guy?" Angela stopped climbing.

"What do you mean?"

"Is he taken or is he fair game?"

"Fair game?"

"Yeah, like, is he your boyfriend?"

"Me? No, not at all. We're friends."

"Are you sure?"

I nodded again.

"Seriously, Jes, because if you're interested I'll stay away. I would never, you know ... encroach."

"He's not my property," I managed a smile. "He's just — Sam."

"A very cute Sam," she nodded, climbing once more. "A little goofy, maybe. But he'd make a good summer boy."

"Summer boy?" I might have gulped at this.

"Just an expression. He seems nice."

Summer boy? Fair game? Blech. That's my favorite word substitute for actually barfing on the spot, and now seemed like an inappropriate time to vomit.

From the look of her set jaw, I'd say hunting season was on and she'd set her sights on Sam.

When we got to the top of the cliff, Dell was getting ready to jump.

"I swear my entire life passes before me every time I grab this rope," she laughed.

"You never know when your number's going to be up," Marshall said, holding the rope for her.

"Well, better kiss me then." Dell smiled dreamily at him.

As they kissed, I looked away. Then I saw Dell's red form hunkered up in her own unique fetal jumping style, outlined against the deep blue of the sky.

"You jumpin' today?" I heard Sam behind me.

"Not today," I answered, as always, but Sam was already moving past me toward Angela. She had unwrapped a towel from her waist and was standing at the highest jumping point with her arms crossed. Sam took the rope, still swinging from Dell's jump, and held it, explaining the theory of jumping in painstaking detail. Angela nodded occasionally. I couldn't tear my eyes away from them. I don't usually think about how Sam looks because mostly he's just Sam, but I couldn't help noticing how good they looked together and the noticing carved a big rip in my insides.

Then Dell called out to Sam. "Did you see my splash?"

"The idea is to get no splash, Dell. Not take half the lake out with you!"

"I like to make a splash! That's the kind of girl I am," she joked back, clinging to Marshall's waist.

Sam turned to Angela and began to repeat the instructions. Angela nodded as though every word glistened with morning dew, shining in the morning sun.

"Thanks, Sam I am," she twinkled up at him, or over to him since she was about the same height. Sam hated it when people pulled the Dr. Seuss thing with his name — asking him if he liked green eggs and ham — but now he just stood there wearing a goofy smile. And for a second I felt a zigzag of jealousy, and then a judo chop of hatred toward Angela. Just like that, out of nowhere. Hatred.

The next thing I knew, Angela pulled back on the rope and without a downward glance, pushed off from the shore and flung herself outward. We all shouted, "Now."

She let go of the rope at the right time, but instead of falling feet first, she managed to twist herself around and dive into the water. Her hands, body, legs and feet entered the water in one fluid motion, making only the barest splash.

Dell, Sam and Marshall stared down at her in disbelief, and then they cheered. Angela's head popped up to the surface and she waved. "I'm here," she shouted, before swimming to the shore with long, sure strokes.

Dell and Angela begged me to have dinner with them at the House of Pizza, but I said Dad was expecting me. Sam went with them, and I noticed he managed to snag a seat beside Angela in the van. I could hear their laughter as they pulled away.

A breeze from the lake sent a chill up my back as I watched the sun dip behind the mountain, bathing the sandy beach in soft, golden tones. Then two arms clutched me from behind and briefly I thought Sam had changed his mind about leaving.

"Jes, come see my mouse house," Danny squinted up at me.

I pushed my disappointment away and let the little boy lead me into the woods. What did I care where Sam had dinner, or who he ate with? He could share a pizza with Godzilla. We were just friends.

Danny kept tugging and chattering about someone named Devon.

"Devon?"

"That's his name."

"Oh, is he a friend from school?"

"Yeah, right. A mouse at school?"

Oops. "Sure, if he's a smart mouse!"

Danny giggled at this. "That's funny. Here! Here it is." He pointed down to a little tepee of twigs and grass. Bits of cheese had been sprinkled around and he'd built a small fence of Popsicle sticks that surrounded the compound.

"Wow, Danny Boy. This is terrific. Did you do this all yourself?"

"Yup. Henry wanted to help, but he always wants to blow it up after, so I never told him where it was."

I looked around to see where, in fact, we were — I'd been paying no attention as Danny had pulled me through the forest. We'd doubled back to the clearing behind our cabin. The willow tree we'd planted eight years ago was only a short distance away and beneath it stood the small white cross, now faded and showing signs of weather. There were blue cornflowers, still fresh, in a vase beside it. Dad.

I left Danny beside his mouse house and heard him coaxing the elusive Devon out of the woods with a piece of cheese. As I approached the tree, it felt like walking back in time to when I was eight years old and we'd come out here, the three of us again. I could see us — Mom and Dad clutching on to each other, and me walking behind. The words on the cross were fading, too, I realized as I drew closer.

Alberta Evelyn Miner-Cooper.

"Alberta? That's her name?" I'd said when they brought her home from the hospital. I'd been horrified. Such an ugly name for such an adorable baby.

"You'll get used to it," Mom had promised, holding me close.

"Your mom wanted to name her for where she grew up," Dad said. "You should be grateful she wasn't born in Saskatchewan or Prince Edward Island!"

Mom had poked him, but we'd laughed. "She's going to love you so much, Jessica. Do you know that? She's going to look up to you and say, 'That's my big sister.'"

Mom had looked so happy that day, shimmering almost, like Mara on a perfect summer morning.

I sat in the dirt now beside the cross and picked a leaf off the gravestone.

"Jes, where ... there you are." Danny trotted over to me. "Devon's not coming. Where do you think he went?"

I shrugged and followed him back to the mouse house.

"He'll be here soon," Danny said confidently. "He's really big. He couldn't get lost. Maybe he's old. Maybe he'll have babies and they'll all live here."

"So he'll have to have a wife, too?" I teased.

"I guess," he said grudgingly. "And we can come see them every year, okay? Forever." He made this pronouncement as he adjusted the Popsicle sticks.

I remembered how it was to think with such certainty that some things could last forever. When I was young, Danny's age probably, and learning about numbers, I had asked my dad how old he was. Thirty-eight, he'd answered. I was awed by that number compared to my measly six years. "When do people die?" I'd asked. He'd said something like, "Oh, sometimes a hundred years, kiddo." A hundred years! That was forever, I'd thought. Really, literally, I thought … I am going to live forever.

When Alberta died, one of the toughest things to grasp was that my dad was wrong. People didn't live forever. I didn't think he had lied to me. It was worse — he hadn't known.

I could still see him, slumped like a chalk outline against the blue wall of the hospital. He had slipped to the ground with his hands over his face and I'd rushed over to him, from my mother's side to his. That was a terrible choice.

Now I felt a small hand make its way into mine. Danny's blue eyes peered up at me. "You're sad," he decided. "It's cuz your little sister died."

"Who told you about that?"

"Sam. He says sometimes you still get sad.

He says it's why you look out across the lake ... sometimes."

I brushed the dirt from my knees and then tousled his blond hair with my hand. "Let's go look for Devon, okay?"

As I followed him to the edge of the woods, I noticed the first star in the evening sky and I wished Sam was here with me.

11

"It wouldn't kill you to be a little nicer to her, Jes." Mom frowned as she took my measurements for the seamstress.

I didn't answer. Partly because I was sucking in my stomach for a more hopeful outcome in the waist measurement, and partly because if I did respond, I would've said something snotty. And I was still trying to make up for my roll-of-quarters comment the other day.

"I am being nice," I managed.

"Nice with your teeth gritted. And don't pull your stomach in so far. You'll be stuck walking around all day looking like a nineteenth-century maiden in a corset."

"That sounds like me," I said. We both laughed, and for a second it felt like old times. Not old, old times, but newer old times, after Dad had moved out. That was awful, but there was a relief as well. I didn't have to wonder when the next fight would break out, or worse, when the next cold spell would settle in.

Mom and I had gotten into our own groove. We watched movies, ate popcorn for dinner and spent a lot of time sitting on the couch close together. It'd been a big shift, but we were together, at least.

When Cal arrived, that was the biggest shift. She stepped over to another plate and I'd been watching her move away ever since.

"After all, Jes, I think she's trying really hard to fit in." Mom's voice brought me back to the present.

Yeah, Angela was fitting in all right. During the last week I'd found her talking on the phone to Dell (though Dell quickly explained that she'd called to talk to me), and the other day she was playing basketball in the backyard with my basketball and Sam when I'd come home from babysitting.

"She's just so ... so ... much," I explained weakly.

"Well, she's had a time of it with her mother, you know. For years she wouldn't even let Angela see Cal."

"How come?" Maybe Cal was a drug dealer.

"It was a messy divorce," she said. My mom liked to distinguish between messy divorces and neat ones. I don't know how many times I'd heard her brag about how amicable her divorce was. The marriage sucked, but they had a very successful divorce.

"I think she could use a friend." Mom pulled the measuring tape down my leg to the floor.

"We don't have anything in common," I argued, staring down at the part in her hair. Except Sam, I could have added. And maybe Dell.

"Just try."

"When I die, I want to be buried in a mall," Angela announced as we stepped through the big revolving doors. Mom had dropped us off to look for shoes and was going to meet us in an hour for lunch.

I checked Angela's face to see what kind of expression would follow a statement like that. She had her head tilted back and was breathing in deeply, the way I did when I first arrived at the lake.

"It's just so clean and organized and hopeful, you know?" Angela said as she strode with those long legs into the middle of the atrium, where hallways spread out like the tentacles of a giant squid.

"Hopeful?" I asked, at least a stride and a half behind.

"Yeah." She slowed a little. "Like everything you need is here. All you have to do is find it!" She said this slowly, looking around. "But I'd change the lighting. I'd definitely change the lighting."

I rubbed my head, confused as usual by this vast expanse of identical storefronts.

But she didn't seem to require a response. She paused at the mall directory, poking a long finger expertly at the little square reassuring us that "you are here."

"Okay, so we start off here ... check out accessories, then move on to shoes and hosiery ... ending with bras. The right bra is crucial. Okay?"

"Check," I said solemnly.

She grabbed my arm and pulled me down one of the squid trails to a department store. We stopped for a breathing break in front of the jewelry counter. A clerk who looked as though her makeup had been applied by a bored undertaker asked if she could help. Angela flashed her movie-star smile and said we were just looking.

"These would look great with the dress, don't you think?" She held a pair of sparkly earrings up against her face.

I shrugged. "Yup."

"Or maybe we should go with pearls. That would be the safe choice, I guess. It's a tough call." She spoke softly and reverently, like she was deciding whether to pull the plug on her Great-Aunt Ethel.

"I'm, uh, just gonna sit down for a second. Take your time." I wandered over to a chair and slumped into it. I felt like we'd been wandering through the desert for hours. I needed water.

I put my elbows on my knees. What a wimp I was. I needed to snap out of it.

"Okay, let's go," Angela said, appearing in front of me, looking very brisk. She almost pushed me out of the store and then pulled me along when I stopped to look at running shoes.

"What's the rush?" I asked.

She didn't answer, didn't say another word until we were back out in the mall, away from the department store. Then she sat down on a bench and fanned her face with her hand. "That was close. Did you see the clerk checking me out? I thought she had me."

"Huh?" I responded dimly.

Angela stole a look around her, then pulled something out of her jacket pocket. The earrings winked up at me and then she pushed them deep into the darkness of her pocket.

"You stole them?" I hissed.

Her eyes flashed. "Shhh. Do you want security to hear you?"

I shook my head as though this was the last thing I wanted. As though I was experienced at avoiding security.

We moved through the mall in silence. Finally she said, "It's just for fun, you know? 'A lark, a spree ... it's very fun, you see.'"

Mary Poppins? Angela was quoting Mary Poppins?

"Your idea of a good time is stealing?"

Her eyebrows rose quickly, up then down again. And her face changed.

"It was stupid ... you're right. I guess I wanted to impress you. Didn't work, I see," she said almost apologetically.

I was uncomfortable. The truth was, something about her daring had impressed me. It took a certain kind of courage —

"It's just wrong," I said. Once the words were out they sounded stupid and naive.

"Well, sure it's wrong, Jes. Jeez. That's the point." She leaned forward and brought the earrings out of her pocket. They glimmered in the palm of her hand. "Lots of things are wrong in the world, don't you think?"

I thought of Alberta's accident, that totally wrong moment in time that had stolen our lives.

"The thing about stealing is that you get to have what you want. Of course, you're scared ... but that's the rush. Doing it anyway."

She made it sound sensible. Almost noble.

"Listen," she continued. "It's not like I do this on a regular basis. And I won't anymore ... not if it makes you uncomfortable." Her green eyes were wide. "Seriously, Jes. I want this to work. I like you."

Okay. It was weird. She'd just stolen a pair of earrings, and I felt like I was being the unreasonable one. It was her face. It was so beautiful ... you almost couldn't believe it could lie. And it wasn't just me ... everybody in the mall was looking at her. Like they couldn't help themselves. Their eyes would move right over me, through me, to get to her. I was invisible. Her looks stopped people, literally arrested them. Odd choice of words. But the thing was, what she had done — stealing — seemed totally opposite of how she looked. The two weren't connected. I knew that. But even though she was guilty ... when you looked at her perfect face, it was hard to not believe in its innocence. It was like you wanted to believe the beauty went right through to the core.

"So you've never shoplifted anything?" she asked as we went to find Mom.

I shook my head.

"Well, I admire that."

I turned to see if she was serious. Her profile glided beside me, bending slightly like Princess Di used to when she wanted to hear what the commoner was saying. I felt like a troll beside her and I grunted, something to the effect of, "Um, well ... it's, you know ..." Typical troll response.

"No, really," she insisted.

So she spoke Troll. Of course she did. She probably got a PhD in "comparative troll and two-headed monsters" just to communicate with the rest of the homely world. Man, I was feeling bitchy. It was oozing out of me in great green, greasy clots of jealousy.

The rest of the shopping trip passed by in a flurry. We bought shoes — ankle breakers — and little purses designed to hold a lipstick and half a tissue. She even talked Mom into buying a two-piece bathing suit. "Of course, you're not too old, Elli. You look fabulous." Slurp, slurp, the sucking up was unbearable. It was like shopping with an anteater.

By the time we were finished, Mom and Angela looked exhilarated, flushed with the hunt, the thrill of a chase written clearly on their faces.

I was bagged and all I could do was droop into the backseat once we finally found our car.

They chatted and giggled all the way home, congratulating each other on their perfect purchases.

"How about you, Jes? Do you like the shoes?" Mom asked.

"I'm so ..." I answered. "It's hard to put it into words."

"Oh, you," she sniffed. "She's like her dad, figures that sneakers and sandals will see her through life."

She's like her dad. Hmm. And Dad was gone now. Gee, you'd have to be brilliant to understand the significance of that. You'd have to be a freaking shrink.

I leaned back against the door. I felt like all my bones had been marinated in vinegar. If shopping was tiring, jealousy was absolutely exhausting.

12

Back home, I snuck outside to the playhouse. I had to bend to get through the door, but it was still roomy enough inside to hold me.

I liked coming here. Dad had put the house together and Mom had helped, even though she was big with being pregnant. I could still see the bulge of her belly. She was handing a plank or something to Dad while he worked on the roof, and I was sitting inside waiting for them to finish. I'd sat in the corner with a couple of stuffed pals, drawing pictures on the walls with colored chalk. Nesting, Mom called it. We were all preparing our nests for the baby. I remember seeing her belly almost fill the doorway and squinting at it. I had imagined the baby inside looking back at me. I'd seen the ultrasound picture, so I knew she was in there and I imagined her making faces at me. (I thought even then that it was a sister.) I made a face back and suddenly the flesh rippled and the baby must have kicked because my mom's hand came down instinctively across the spot. I heard her laughter, and she said something to my dad with a voice as soft and rippling as a waterfall. But I knew the baby was waving at me.

A tear slid down my cheek now. As I wiped it away, a face appeared in the small window.

"Can I come in and play?" Dell's voice filled the small space.

"If you can fit."

I was happy to see her. The lonely feeling slipped away as she bent herself into a sitting position beside me.

"Remember when we used to play with our Barbies out here?" she asked.

"Yeah."

"I wanted them to go to proms and balls ..."

"I made them join the army and fight in the Gulf War!"

We both laughed.

"You were so bossy," Dell said.

"Me? You're the one who made sure their shoes matched their army fatigues. High heels to war?"

"You can never be too well dressed."

"You sound like your mother," I said.

"Ouch." She held her hand over her heart as though she'd been mortally wounded. "What are you doing out here anyway?"

"The house has been taken over ... occupied by Angela and Mom. Wedding Storm, I'm calling it.

You should see it in there, Dell, honestly."

She shrugged. "Sounds like fun to me. Weddings are so romantic." Her eyes went soft and mushy, and I knew she was thinking about Marshall.

"Your Barbies were always getting married."

"And yours always showed up to protest when the minister asked, 'Does anyone object?' Hmm, that's interesting, don't you think, Jes?"

"Oh, please. No more analysis," I groaned, flopping down on the rough floor.

"I'm just saying," her voice rose suggestively, then lowered to normal, "one of these days you're going to have to get used to the idea."

I sat up again. "Don't you think it's curious, though, that whenever the couple gets together in fairy tales and they live — supposedly — happily ever after, that's the *end* of the story?"

"So?"

"So! So, Adele, the story never *starts* that way ... with the prince or whoever carrying his bride over the threshold. I mean, you never actually *see* anyone living happily ever after."

She groaned.

"No, I'm serious. Not one fairy tale ever shows that part and yet ... yet ..." My voice crescendoed. "That's what we're supposed to believe. I think it's a big conspiracy!"

"And who are the conspirors ... conspirators ... whatever?"

"I don't know. Hans Christian Andersen, The Brothers Grimm ... Mother Goose! I don't know. Whoever writes these things — Disney. The point is ..." I faded.

"Yeah? The point is what?"

"There's no happily ever after."

"Poo!"

I smiled. Dell always said that when she couldn't think of anything else. "Good comeback."

"You're such a ... a ... love grinch. Yeah. The Grinch Who Stole ... the Happy Ending. That's your fairy tale."

"That was Doctor Seuss."

"Whatever. Anyway, Angela said you guys found the most awesome shoes, so maybe you just need to scale down your happy-ending expectations," she said. "You know what my mom always says — 'the shoes make the outfit.'"

"You talked to Angela?" I asked. A steel shaft of fear pierced my heart. "When?"

"Oh," she stopped smiling and looked guilty, which made the hole widen inside me.

"Just now. I called to talk to you, but Angela answered," Dell over-explained, which made me feel worse, not better. "That's okay, right?"

"Of course it is. She likes you, Dell ... thinks you're cool."

"It's no big deal, Jes. It's not a Sara thing."

When we'd gone to junior high, a girl named Sara had started hanging out with us. We'd both really liked her. She was loud and funny and, as we discovered eventually, the biggest liar in the western hemisphere. We'd included her in everything we did and it was a lot of fun at first. Then she started saying little things about Dell when she wasn't there and, I found out later, was doing the same thing about me. It seemed pretty innocent at first. But then she'd say, "Maybe I shouldn't say this, but I thought you'd want to know ... Dell thinks you're too much of a tomboy." Or, "Jes thinks your stories aren't very good." Stuff like that. It almost tore us apart until we talked. When we confronted Sara about it, she denied the whole thing. She called us losers and trotted off to make friends with Alice Birch. Good riddance, we'd said. But it scared both of us.

I smiled, relieved. "I know. You're right. I'm trying to get used to her, honestly."

"It must be weird, though," Dell said comfortingly. "But it might not be all bad. She's pretty fun." She tried to stand, but it was impossible. "Come on. I'm cramping up here."

"In a minute. You go in."

"Are you sure?"

"Yeah. I just want to check and see if Sam's around."

She brightened. "Good idea!"

I held out my arm. "Not one word," I ordered as I followed her out of the playhouse.

In the sunshine she stretched out her long limbs. "I'm just saying … when those braces come off? Watch out!"

"Argh," I said before moving the loose plank out of the way and squeezing through to Sam's backyard. I could hear Dell's laughter as I walked toward his house. She was so wrong about Sam and me, but nothing I ever said could change her mind.

"Hey, Jes." Danny was in his sandbox building a smaller version of his lake castle. "Mom and me are making a dungeon. You can, too."

Amber's lawn chair was spread out beside him, and with her beach umbrella, iced tea and open book across her chest, she didn't look too industrious.

"Your mom looks like she's got everything under control," I joked.

Amber's eyes peered up at me between the brim of her hat and her sunglasses. "I'm supervising."

"Sam home?"

"In his darkroom, hon. Just knock first."

"I know the drill. Thanks."

I let myself in the house and walked down the stairs to the basement. I tapped twice with sharp, distinct knocks. He knocked back once. There was a pause and then two more knocks. I tapped three times in succession. It was our code, but today it annoyed me. As he was completing the code, I yelled, "Just let me in!"

The door opened a crack. "You're grouchy today," he said.

"I've already been called a grinch and forced to buy high-heeled shoes. Nothing you say can touch me."

He reached out his hand and touched my hair like I was a poodle. "You're so fierce."

"Believe it," I said shortly. Then I saw the pictures he was developing. "Sam, they're beautiful," I said, impressed as usual by his skill.

"They're okay. You think?" There was pride in his voice and doubt. I liked the combination.

I looked closely at the series — more lake pictures. He already had countless photos of the lake dating back ten or so years when he first took up photography. And they kept getting better as his skill increased. He managed to capture the lake in all its moods. Flat and motionless, violet and shimmering, gray and ferocious in the midst of a summer storm. I never tired of looking at his pictures. "Oh, Sam," I said softly.

"Yeah, yeah," he said, sounding embarrassed, but pleased.

"Check this one out. It's part of my Jes series. My Jes-in-baseball-cap series." He held out an eight by ten of me taken the other day when we were fishing.

It was a head shot and my eyes were shaded by the brim of the cap, and all around was the brilliant cobalt sky. I'd forgotten what a stunning day it had been. I looked happy. I liked it.

"It looks just like me," I said, handing it back to him. "How do you do that? All the pictures my mom takes of me look like someone else."

He shrugged. "Sometimes you tense up on film, especially when someone says, 'Smile.' You don't like anyone telling you what to do. You just sort of vacate your body, then ... I'm not sure where you go."

"Okay, okay," I laughed. "What is this, 'Analyze Jes' day? You and Dell."

"You're just so mysterious."

"And you're so full of it," I answered. Then I caught sight of a picture he'd taken of my dad. "Is it dry?"

Sam nodded.

I unclipped the peg and held the picture in my hands. Sam had caught my dad unaware, without the usual half-smile he wore in photos. His eyes were bright blue, brighter still because of all the blue around us — holding sky and water. But it was the sadness in them that made me take a sharp breath. I could barely look at it, yet I couldn't take my eyes away. It was like you could see all the way inside him.

"I know," was all Sam said. And I knew he did. "You can have it," he added.

I wasn't sure that I wanted it, but I took it all the same. I knew I didn't want anyone else to have it. I could stick it in a drawer somewhere. I didn't have to look at it again.

Sam put it in an envelope. "So it won't get creased," he said as he handed it to me. "Are you and your dad going up for the corn festival?"

"Yeah, I guess. Next weekend, right?"

He nodded, then turned back to a picture still bathing in solution.

"Boy, the summer is flying," I said, peering over his shoulder. He moved slightly, his broad shoulders blocking my view. "What?" I said, trying to squeeze past him. "What don't you want me to see?"

Sometimes being little comes in handy, and I maneuvered my way in front of him. I looked down and there, in full, although water-blurred, was a close-up of Angela. She was standing on the bluff gazing out at the lake.

"It's a good picture," I said, generously I thought.

"Yeah, I got some nice ones of Dell and Marshall, too," he said quickly. Too quickly. "Want to see them?"

"Why didn't you want me to see this one?" I asked.

Sam looked embarrassed — maybe he even

blushed, although in this light it was hard to tell. "I don't care ... it's not finished," he muttered.

"Which one?" I persisted. "You don't care, or it's not finished?" *Bulldog,* I could hear Dell say. *Get lost,* I thought.

Then he held up his hands, palms up. "I don't know, Jes. You're so ... weird about her."

This hit me like a punch to the gut. I turned to leave. I wanted to get out.

"No, don't go," he said. "That's not what I meant."

"Yes, it is. It's exactly what you meant. Don't make it worse by lying."

"Lying? Give me a break, Jes." His hand covered mine on the doorknob as he tried to stop me from pulling the door open.

I went a little ballistic then. I shook his hand off, because I felt trapped, and I pulled the door open abruptly. "So then take a break. Take all the time you need," I shouted, making no sense at all. As I walked up the stairs, I heard him yank the door shut. What I really wanted was for him to follow me. I moved slowly, my version of waiting, but the only thing that followed me was basement silence, humming water boilers and the whir of the washing machine.

"That was fast," Amber said as I came out the back door. "Is he lost in his art?"

"Something like that," I mumbled.

"You want some iced tea or a soda?" she asked.

"Nah. I should get home."

"Keep me company, Jes. Danny ran off with that little girl down the street ... the Kennedy girl."

"Lucy?"

"That's the one. Oh, well," she said, sipping her tea. "It has to happen sooner or later, I guess. I might as well get used to it."

I sat down on the corner of the sandbox and absently patted Danny's sand creation.

"That's why I wanted a daughter. They don't leave quite the same way. But I guess I was meant to raise sons."

"I guess," I said. I packed some sand into a pail and wetted it down with Danny's water gun. Then I turned it upside down, making a perfectly formed mound of sand.

"Your mom's pretty busy these days."

"Yup."

"I miss her a little."

"But you talk all the time!"

"It's different now."

"Tell me about it." I packed more sand into the pail.

"But he's a nice guy, Cal. I like him." Amber poured herself some more iced tea. "You sure you don't want any?"

I shook my head.

"Do you like him?"

"Sure, yeah. What's not to like?" I really didn't want to get into this with her. It would be like pouring information directly into a funnel leading to my mother.

"You can talk to me if you want, Jes. I'm not such a big blabbermouth."

"Do all moms read minds?" I asked.

"Oh, for sure. It's in the manual. It's one of the first things you learn after diaper protocol and burping techniques."

I stretched out on the grass. "It's not him, Amber. I mean he's not a pervert or anything."

"High praise."

"It's just that everything's different. She's different ... we're different ..." I trailed off.

"How?"

"It just happened, like, overnight. One day we were us, and then one day we weren't anymore." I didn't think I was making much sense, but Amber was nodding.

"I know. One day she was needing us and then one day she wasn't." Her eyes were hidden behind sunglasses. "Everything changes, Jes. That's just life. Sometimes we have to let go of who we think someone is before we can really see them — see who they're becoming. But it's hard to let go."

This was disappointing. And confusing. I turned the pail over and the sand struggled for a second to retain its shape, but there wasn't enough water and it crumbled.

I wiped my hands on my pants, felt the residual sand slip off. "I should go."

"You can talk to me anytime," I heard her say as I pulled the fence plank aside. A vine brushed my face and I smelled its faint perfume as I climbed through to my yard.

13

"So, what's it like, living in California?" Dell was asking as I entered the room. "Hey, Jes," she added as she saw me.

"Hey," I said, slipping the envelope with Dad's photo into my nightstand drawer, hoping that Dell wouldn't notice. But she was staring, her jaw in her hands, at Angela.

"It's great," Angela answered, frowning slightly as she reached to put polish on her toenails.

"I want to write a screenplay one day," Dell said.

Angela's head lifted. "I was in a movie."

"What? No way." Dell's eyes widened.

Angela smiled like she was holding on to a juicy secret. But only for a second. "A couple, actually. It was just extra work, but it's a start. I'm going to be an actress. I want to be a Bond girl."

"Wow. That's interesting, isn't it, Jes?" Dell swerved around on the bed and grabbed my foot. But before I could answer she spun around again on her bum, legs lifted, and then curved into a cross-legged position, gazing at Angela. She looked like an eager pupil sitting at the foot of one of those kung-fu masters. "Tell us about it."

"Well, one of them was barely a walk-on, but in my most recent film, I got to sit in the bleachers at a horse race and the star was, like, two feet away from me."

"Who?" Dell asked breathlessly.

Angela paused. "You know Chad Grimes?"

Dell blanched — literally turned white. "You are totally lying now!"

Angela grinned.

"Who is, uh, he?" I asked, a little curious.

"Oh, Jes." Dell spun again, her red curls flying in her face. "*The Daring and the Dashing?*"

"Huh?"

"It's a soap opera. He's the most gorgeous guy on the show. Dark Lansing."

"Dark? That's his name?" I laughed. "Dell, you could come up with a better name than that!"

She ignored me. "He played twins last year. In this one story line, his evil twin kidnaps him and then takes over his identity and starts living with the good twin's wife until she suspects, right? But then she gets amnesia and falls in love with him for real."

"He's got a major gift," Angela agreed seriously, as she applied a second coat of polish.

"So, did you get to talk to him?" Dell asked.

"Nah. We're not supposed to talk to the talent."

"That's what they're called?" I said. "The talent?"

"Uh-huh. But he was watching me. I could tell and it really, you know, inspired my performance."

"What did you have to do?" Dell asked.

"We were at a horse race so we had to cheer, and when it was my turn, well, I gave him something to watch," she said mysteriously. "When I left, I asked one of the prop guys to give him my head shot, but he probably didn't."

Dell's jaw dropped and I couldn't bear it anymore. If I didn't stop this, she'd be asking Angela for her autograph.

"Dell's an amazing writer," I offered. "She's writing a novel."

Dell reddened. "More like a novella."

"At three hundred pages? I don't think so. It's so great. It's this science-fiction story where —"

"You have to let me read it one day," Angela broke in eagerly. "I know people who might be interested in it." Then she laughed. "That sounded pretentious, didn't it? But seriously ... maybe it could be turned into a movie. You never know. Is there a part in it for me?" A glorious smile followed this.

"Wow," said Dell.

"Good word," I mumbled.

"Oh, Jes," Angela said suddenly. "I forgot to tell you, Mrs. Kennedy called."

"How is Mrs. Black Forest doing?" Dell asked.

"What's that?" Angela asked.

Dell grinned. "It's the mother cake-rating method Jes and I made up. Mrs. Kennedy's a Black Forest mom. All whipped cream and chocolate shavings on the outside ... looks really good, but when you take a bite, all you can taste is that awful liqueur stuff."

I nodded. "Sam's mom, Amber, is double chocolate fudge. What you see is what you get."

"My mom's vanilla with a lemon glaze. Kind of tart and sour but solid inside. Elli is German chocolate."

"Yeah," I said. "Good cake on the inside, but it has all that caramel, coconut icing ..."

Dell took over. "Kind of sweet, but let's face it ..."

We both said the last part together. "... a little nutty." We laughed.

"What kind is your mom?" Dell asked Angela.

Angela just shrugged, but Dell persisted. "C'mon."

She looked up from polishing her toenails and tilted her head to the side. "The kind with a file in it."

Dell and I exchanged glances.

"How come?" I asked.

"Oh, I don't know." For a second Angela's face went still, like she was weighing thoughts. "She never wanted kids," she said finally.

"Really?" Dell leaned forward. "But then she had you, right? So she changed her mind." Dell flung her hands out in a dramatic gesture. "Couldn't imagine life without you."

Angela just looked at her. "Yeah, that's probably what she meant when she said she wished I'd never been born."

Dell didn't have anything to say to this, and the room fell silent.

"Dell loves happy endings," I said quietly.

Angela shrugged and got up from the bed, walking almost ducklike with those sponge things between her toes. She pulled a drawer open.

"Major change of subject," she announced. She drew a scarf out of the drawer. It was flimsy and fringed at the edges. "I don't know why I bought this." She went over to Dell and placed it around her shoulders. "But I think it's a perfect writing shawl, don't you?"

Dell squealed and wrapped herself in it. "It's silk," she exclaimed, brushing the soft fabric against her face. Then she glanced at the price tag, still attached. "Angela, I can't take this. It's too beautiful. Too expensive."

Angela shook her head. "I get way too much money for that extra work. Besides, the color makes me look jaundiced. I cannot wear yellow for the life of me."

I was nursing a flicker of suspicion as to how

that scarf might have really come into Angela's possession, when the door opened and Mom poked her head into the room.

"Hi, Dell," she said. "Can I see you for a minute, Jes?" Then she left.

"I'll be right back," I said, but Dell had already returned to the subject of Chad Grimes, with the swath of silk wrapped tightly around her.

I ran my hand across the wall as I walked to Mom's room, remembering when she and I had painted it. Dad had just moved out and Mom and I were doing everything together. The color was bright yellow, although the paint store guy refused to call it that. Mexican Sunshine, he'd called it. "Time to cheer things up," Mom had said.

Between my room and my mom's was Alberta's room. The nursery. I cracked open the door and looked inside. It was empty. The crib and change table had been given away. The walls were a dusty rose, and they still held all the sadness. I closed it tightly and went into Mom's room.

She was at her writing desk. She smiled as I entered. "Hi, sweetie. Sit down."

I sat at the edge of her bed. "What's up?"

"I just needed your opinion on a few things."

There was a stack of magazines beside the bed. Billowy, powder-puff brides on the covers mostly. I picked one up and started flicking through it.

"Shoot," I said.

"Well, the church we'd planned to use just called and said there was a mistake and they're double-booked."

"So you have to cancel the wedding?" I asked.

Mom sighed. "Yes. That's the only solution I can come up with." Her sharp eyes lasered into mine. "Oh well, can't say I didn't give it a shot." Her voice was heavy with sarcasm and it made me laugh.

She looked relieved.

"So, find another church."

"I could do that, but I was thinking. Amber offered us the clubhouse up at the lake. What do you think? It would be beautiful."

My heartbeat doubled as I saw my last refuge being taken away. There really would be no place to hide if Mom and Cal chose the lake and made it theirs. But I forced myself to sound calm. "I thought you hated it up there."

"Jessica, how can you say that? Some of our best times were ..." she stopped abruptly. "Maybe it is a bad idea. I just thought it would be pretty and ..."

"And?"

"And I'd be closer to Alberta." Her voice was so quiet, I could barely hear her.

All the hardness I was feeling crumbled when I heard her say that. We'd buried Alberta's ashes there. Another time, I would have run directly into her arms and held on. I knew how comforting it would feel ... warm and safe. But I couldn't.

"Then you should do it, Mom," I said, clutching the quilt on her bed with tight fists. Anything I'd ever felt about my little sister always shrunk away next to my mother's great loss.

"I want you to be okay with it."

I wanted to shout, "I'm not okay with it ... any of it." But instead I just said, "Whatever. It's your wedding."

She took a step toward me like she was going to hug me, but I backed up and she stopped. Tears filled her eyes.

"Jes, what's happening to us?"

"Nothing." I shook my head quickly. "I'm, uh ... Dell's over. I should get back."

"We have to talk." She sat down again, gave me some space.

"It won't change anything, will it? You've made your decision. It doesn't matter where or when, not really. I'll be there. What more do you want?" My voice was high and shaky. I didn't sound like me at all. It was like I was outside of the whole thing. Outside of my own life looking in through the crack of a closing door.

"Cal's a good man, Jes. He makes me happy."

"And Dad's not a good man?" I shouted. The shift shocked us both, I think.

Mom looked as though I'd slapped her. "He's made his choices, too, Jes." Her voice was shaky.

"What kind of choices? You made him leave. He didn't want to go." I was shaking.

"Listen to me, Jessica, please. When Alberta died a tidal wave hit this family. I clung on to you … maybe too much. I don't know. But I couldn't lose you, too."

"So you lost Dad instead?"

She held her hand up. "Your father, he … clung as well, but not to me."

I didn't understand what she was saying. Not at first and not from her words. But her face told me everything. The way her eyes shifted down to her hands, to her left hand. Then it hit me with the same force as the tidal wave she talked about.

"What are you saying?"

But she wouldn't look up at me. Twisting the ring on her finger, she whispered in words almost too low to hear, "He found someone else."

I think I said, "You're lying," before I left the room. All I remembered later was that I ran through the yellow hallway that laughed at me, past the closed door and outside into the glaring sunshine. And then I was lost.

I don't know how I made it to my father's apartment. He buzzed me in, and when I reached his apartment door, it was wide open.

"Come in," he yelled from his bedroom.

He was sitting on the bed with blueprints in front of him.

"Hey, Funny Face, good to see you."

"What are you doing?" I asked, breathing heavily from the run over.

"The Crukshanks are remodeling their summer house — the one at the north end of the lake? They want me to take the job, but I don't know. What's up with you? Did you run all the way?"

I realized I was still having trouble getting my breath. "I just need to, uh, use the bathroom," I said, ducking into the small room.

I leaned against the door and tried to imagine telling him what Mom had said. But in that instant I knew I didn't want to hear the answer, any answer. I wanted to never have had that conversation with my mother.

When I came out, he was waiting in the living room. He was wearing jeans and an old red T-shirt. As he pulled his hands through his hair with the morning stubble still on his face, I realized he was a handsome man. I wondered if I'd ever noticed this before. I must have.

Suddenly I could imagine someone else seeing him ... but not as my dad, and I almost felt nauseous.

"What's up, Funny Face?"

As familiar as this nickname was for me, and the red shirt and the way he pulled at his hair — he looked like a stranger. I rushed over and hugged him tightly.

He didn't say anything at first, just patted my hair with his hand.

"What's up?" His voice was so low it barely registered.

Everything, I could have said. Everything is up, floating around me like gravity just quit. And I had no idea how, or if, anything would ever come down to earth again.

"Are we still going up to the lake this weekend?" I asked.

"When have we ever missed the Amazing Maze of Maize?"

A little piece of yesterday settled back to earth, and I grabbed it gratefully.

"That's what I thought. I just wanted to check."

"Are you okay?" He said, taking a step back to look at me.

I nodded, and it was a lie. I didn't know if I'd ever be okay again. Not in the same way. This was changing me.

14

The Amazing Maze of Maize was a corn festival with clowns and a few carnival rides and a big red-and-white striped tent, which housed barbecues and ice-cream stands. It was kind of lame, and I loved it. We came every year.

The drill was that each group of "mazers" carried a flag on a pole so that if you got lost in the maze, all you had to do was raise your flag and someone — usually a clown — would come and rescue you. Of course, it was totally humiliating if you had to be rescued and it had never happened to me. I could always find my way out.

Dad and I had driven up the night before and had had a quiet dinner down by the lake. While he'd cleaned up, I did some star spinning on the beach. That's a game we play at Mara. What you do is choose your star, fix your eyes on it, spread your arms as wide as you can, and twirl and twirl until the only thing you can see is the narrow pinprick of light. The trees and sky become one, and that beacon of light holds you until you fall to the sand, unable to spin anymore. The other part of the game is be so dizzy that you stumble around, crashing into other star spinners. But I like to slow my spin until the trees and sky part again and I'm still held inside that narrow shaft of light. I like to think that some of the brightness goes inside me, because I've heard that by the time a star's light reaches the earth, the star has already burned out. It makes me feel good to think that I carry some of that extinguished light.

"Jes, over here," Dell's voice rang out from across the maze field. She had left a message that her dad would be bringing Marshall, Angela and her up for the day. We should meet at ten o'clock, she said. I wasn't surprised that Angela was coming. She was part of us now.

Dell rushed over and gave me a big hug. I hugged her back.

"Where have you been? I've left messages all week!"

"Babysitting, mostly. And staying at my dad's."

"You're not avoiding me?"

I shook my head, but I couldn't bring myself to say anything. Maybe I had been avoiding her a little.

"Jes?" She was persistent.

"It's just Wedding Storm."

"Oh, that. Well, Angela is pretty psyched, isn't she?"

"Yeah, where is she?"

"Over there. Talking to Marshall. Is Sam here yet?"

"I haven't seen him."

"Oh." A heavy silence fell between us. "Is it okay with you?" she asked eventually.

"Is what okay?"

"Angela and Sam."

My stomach flipped. "For the millionth time, Sam and I are just friends, Dell," I said. "What about them?" I couldn't help myself.

"I think they're sort of going out. Sort of. She said it was okay with you … that you'd talked."

"Yeah, we talked," I said. "It doesn't matter. We're just friends," I repeated, and the "just" sounded totally piddly and useless. Like it couldn't measure up to anything.

She didn't argue like she would have in the past. In fact, she looked relieved. "Okay, good."

I started to walk over to the tent, but Dell held me back.

"What?" I said.

"It's just, well, I wanted to say something before, but you haven't been around."

"So?"

"Would you, um, could you maybe not talk about my — you know, my writing stuff here?"

"Sure," I shrugged.

"It's just that it's no big deal, you know? And

Marshall and I, we agree that maybe I need to work on some changes."

"Changes?"

"Yeah, like that stupid novel I've been writing. It's not really working."

"Dell, it's a great novel. Great! And you're a great writer!" I said this loudly, explosively almost.

Dell grabbed my arm and pulled me over to a tree, out of view of the others. Her face was serious.

"It was kid stuff, Jes. Marshall, I mean, he's a great writer. He says that if you can't say something concisely, like in a poem, it's just a waste of words." She pulled a small strip of bark off the tree trunk with her nails. "Three hundred and fifty pages and I'm not even halfway through! Who am I kidding?"

I was speechless.

"I mean, Marshall's really talented." She pulled a wider strip off the tree, leaving the soft white wood exposed like a wound. "Angela thinks so, too."

"But you've always wanted to — dreamed of being a writer, Dell."

"Kid stuff," she said again, not looking at me.

"Stop saying that!"

"But it's true. We have to grow up eventually."

"Oh, Dell." I put my hand on her back, but she moved away abruptly.

"Let's go, okay? I don't want to talk about this. I —" Her eyes were bright with tears that were threatening to spill over. "Is my mascara okay?"

"Uh, yeah."

"Come," she ordered, and I followed her.

As we drew closer to the tent, I noticed that Sam and his family had arrived. Danny and Henry were racing around causing their usual havoc with water pistols. Geoff was trying to herd them and Amber looked unperturbed — an island in their midst — with a cup of coffee cradled in her hands.

I was about to say hello, when I saw Sam walk up to Angela and Marshall. As she turned to greet him, her face changed and she reached over and kissed him on the lips like she belonged there.

Everything seemed to go dark around the edges. It was like star spinning — I couldn't look away. They looked so good together. And then gradually the world began to move again.

I saw Amber's face darken. In my peripheral vision, I could see Dell's concerned look. Angela peeked over Sam's shoulder straight at me. Was it defiance? Victory in her eyes? I didn't know. My concentration was focused on only one thing: show nothing.

I didn't even feel myself move toward them. Dell must have guided me because her hand was on my elbow, taking me to the last place on earth I wanted to be.

"Hi, Jes!" Angela said brightly.

I thought Sam moved away from her side when he saw me. "Hey, Elf," he said, too cheerfully.

Marshall grunted a hello, maybe in an effort to conserve words.

Angela walked up to me and engulfed me, troll that I was, in a brief, exuberant hug.

"This is too sweet!" Angela gushed, spinning around. "The Amazing Maze of Maize ... too adorable."

"If you like puns," Marshall said.

"Party pooper," she teased, flipping her hair over her shoulder, a gesture that said, "Oh, what a burden all this long glorious hair is." I thought I saw Marshall blush a little, and something unusual crossed his dour exterior. Oh, a smile!

"Here's our flag, Jes." Danny rushed up and thrust the pole into my hands. I took it numbly. "Are you ready to go?"

"Not this year, Shrimp," Sam said firmly. "You go with Mom and Dad."

"No way. Dad's barbecuing and Mom always gets lost."

Amber had joined the group as well. "I'll try to concentrate this time, Danny. The big kids want to go by themselves." She said this to her son, but I knew she was talking to me. I couldn't look at her.

"It's okay. I'll go with him," I said.

"See?" Danny pushed his way to my side.

"No, Jes, we want you to come with us," Sam said adamantly. Dell and Angela backed him up.

Amber tried to take Danny's hand, but he was firmly attached to my side. He looked down at the ground stubbornly and I could tell he was trying not to cry.

"Really, you guys, it's okay. Danny Boy and I, we're a team. I don't think I could even figure this thing out without him."

"Yeah," he echoed loudly, brushing his eyes with the back of his sleeve.

"Crybaby," Henry muttered as he walked by with a group of his friends.

"Shut up," Danny exploded, and would have torn off after him if I hadn't held fast.

"Listen, we better go. We'll meet you at the ice-cream stand afterward," I said.

"Are you sure?" Amber asked as Danny pulled me away. I nodded over my shoulder.

We entered the maze and I felt relief as the tall cornstalks surrounded us. All you could see was row upon row of corn leaning elegantly with the wind, and the deep blue above.

"Do you want to hold the flag?" I asked.

He grabbed it excitedly and moved quickly up the first path. "Hurry."

"There's no rush," I said, following him. We could stay here all morning and it would suit me fine.

He slowed and took my hand. It felt warm and moist. "I know how to go, Jes."

"It's different every year."

"Can we do this forever, Jes? You and me?"

"Sure," I said, thinking back to that kiss. Sam and Angela together.

"Promise? Forever? Jes?"

"Let's go this way," I said, taking a sudden turn.

"Okay," he agreed happily. His hand left mine as he trudged ahead.

I tried to concentrate on the twists and turns of the maze, but all I could see was that kiss. The flutter of her hair. Sam's tall, straight back. His willingness. The faint color in her cheeks. The look in her eyes as they met mine.

We turned a corner and she was suddenly there, locked in an embrace. The ground seemed to grind beneath me and I grabbed a stalk of corn for support. It rustled loudly and Angela moved back at the sound.

Two faces stared back at me, but I ducked quickly down another trail.

Before Angela and Marshall could say a word.

15

It took a full minute for me to realize that Danny was no longer with me. Everything else fled my mind as panic set in. I called out his name. There was no answer. He has the flag, I told myself. But he was so little.

I moved through the maze quickly, I didn't know which path to take. The lump tightened inside me as I breathed heavily, almost running now. I moved past a group and asked them if they'd seen a little blond boy. I heard their "no" faintly and moved on. Finally I made myself stop and listen. All that mattered was finding his little hand again. "Please, please," I whispered as I turned a corner. And there he was, standing as tall as he could with his flag held high. It barely grazed the top of the tallest stalk.

"Oh, Jes." His face folded into tears and the flag came crashing down beside him. He rushed into my arms, almost knocking me over. "You were lost," he whispered into my ear.

"I'm so sorry, Danny. I shouldn't have let go."

He snuffled against me, and I rubbed his bony back until the shudders subsided.

"I'm not crying," he said, taking a big gulp of air.

I smiled down at his tearful, dirt-streaked face. I didn't argue.

"Are you ready to go now?" I asked.

"Uh-huh."

"Well, grab the flag, Danny Boy."

He didn't let go of my hand until we were standing safely outside the exit of the maze. I thought Amber looked relieved to see us. Everyone else was ordering ice cream.

"Everything okay?" she asked, kneeling to wipe Danny's dirty face with her untucked shirt.

"Mom," he jerked away, embarrassed.

"Sorry," she sighed, standing again. She watched the little boy race over to the ice-cream stand, shouting to anyone within earshot about how I'd gotten lost and how he'd found me.

Amber's eyes weren't missing a thing.

"I'm sorry, Amber. I stopped for a second and then he was gone —"

"Don't worry about it. If I had a quarter for every time I lost one of those monsters ..." She smiled. "He's in such a hurry to catch up to his brothers, to be one of the big kids."

"It's overrated," I said, looking over at the group.

"You want some ice cream?" she asked.

"Nah." I wondered if responding to life's problems with ice cream was also in the mother's manual. "I think I'll see if Dad wants to go now."

"He's helping Geoff with the barbecue. Why don't you walk back to the campground with me? I could use the exercise." She grimaced down at her wide hips.

I nodded.

"I'll go tell them."

"I'll wait by the road," I said, pointing to a bench far away from the ice-cream stand.

Dell was waving me to come over, but I shook my head.

"I've gotta go back," I shouted.

She rushed over, even though I motioned for her to stay where she was.

"What's up? We're going to the Ferris wheel. Come with us."

"Listen, five's a crowd. You guys go. I'm ... tired." That was lame and Dell knew it.

"You're tired? Jes, we can do three in a seat. You're so little." She tried teasing.

I groaned. "I don't feel like it, okay?"

She glanced over to the others. Angela was laughing attractively at something Sam had said. Barf. He'd never said anything that funny in his life.

"She does sort of lay it on a bit thick with him," Dell whispered.

If you only knew, I thought, remembering that

passionate cornfield kiss. It made the earlier one with Sam look like a birthday kiss from an ancient aunt.

"She's got a lot of energy. I'll say that for her."

"I feel terrible leaving you," she said, clarifying that she wasn't going to offer to come with me. To choose me.

"I'm gonna go for a swim. I'll see you later."

"Okay." She sounded reluctant, but she left.

"Are you ready?" Amber asked.

I followed her up to the road. I tried not to think of how pathetic it was that I was spending a Saturday afternoon with my best friend's mother. Or was it ex-best friend?

"Let's take the path," I said, ducking into the tall trees. Amber followed with a heavy crunch.

"Embarrassed to be seen with me, huh?"

"Totally," I answered and she laughed, scaring a couple of birds out of their nest.

"Are you sure you won't get lost?" she asked, after we'd gone deeper into the woods.

"I only get lost when I'm in charge of little boys," I answered apologetically.

She chuckled at this. "He worships you," she said.

"Who?" I blurted and then cursed myself.

"Danny," she clarified as if it was a reasonable question. "So, tell me a little about this Angela person." Her tone changed, like a mother bear would sound if she could speak.

"She's, uh, fine."

"Well, your mother says she's been helpful and all that, but then she's seeing things through a haze of wedding dust these days. It's good, though, to see her so —"

"Happy. I know," I said bluntly. We continued walking in silence. Amber's heavy breathing filled the gap, and then we were through the trees. The lake lay sprawled out in front of us, winking and gleaming in the afternoon sun.

"Could you slow down a little? I'm not thirty anymore."

I stopped to let Amber catch her breath.

She sat down on a stump. "Okay, I'm not even forty anymore," she grinned.

"You're not even forty-two —" I started to say, but she held out an arm and scowled. I laughed.

"What happened in the cornfield?" she asked, gazing out at the lake. "I might lose track of my kids once in a while. You never do."

A seagull squawked loudly beside us, a crust of bread lodged in its beak. I watched it struggle for a better hold, but it dropped it onto the gray pebbled shore. Boat fumes wafted in with the breeze.

"Okay, hypothetical situation," I said.

"Absolutely," she agreed.

I faced her. "You wouldn't be able to tell anyone, not a soul."

She looked hesitant.

"Never mind," I said.

"Okay. Agreed. Not a soul, although if it's a hypothetical situation —"

"Not a soul."

She held an arm across her chest solemnly. "I promise."

"Okay." I took a deep breath. I had to tell someone. "What if you saw your best friend's boyfriend in a ... kissing situation with your other best friend's, uh ..." I couldn't bring myself to say *girlfriend*. "... person in their life?"

Amber started to laugh, but squelched it almost immediately. "Sorry, that was a little confusing — 'other best friend's person in their ...'" Then her eyes widened. "Angela and that Marshall guy? That little witch! I mean, that hypothetical little —"

"Well, Marshall didn't look like he was exactly resisting."

"Humph."

She made a camel noise.

"I don't know what to do. Do I tell Dell and Sam?"

Amber was still looking like a mother bear. "I could tell them."

"No, Amber. You promised!" I was horrified that

Sam might find out I told his mom before him. "I shouldn't have said anything."

"No, Jes. Relax. I won't. Oh, I hate this part about being a mother. I can't tell you how much easier it was to kiss a scraped knee."

"I'm sorry I told you, Amber. I wasn't even thinking about that part of it."

"Don't be sorry. I'm glad you told me. I have to get used to being on the outside of their lives, as much as I hate it."

The waves lapped softly against the stones. Usually the sound filled me, but today there wasn't any room.

"It's hard watching your kids grow up, knowing that they need you less and less," Amber said.

"Sometimes it's the other way around," I mumbled, picking up a flat rock and sending it skipping into the water.

"I guess it feels that way right now, doesn't it? Like your mother is going her own way?"

I didn't answer.

"I think I know how you feel." She sat down on a log.

"No offense, Amber, but I don't think you do. I mean, I know the boys are changing and stuff, but you guys have it made, really. You're a perfect family."

"There's no such thing, Jes."

I couldn't believe she'd said that. She did have it

made. Her husband adored her, so did her boys —
no matter what she said. I felt let down.

"Really, Jes. This whole notion of the perfect
family, it's like a … an urban myth. Like the story
of the guy with the hook scraping the car door on
the lonely highway."

The look on my face made her laugh.

"Okay, bad example. But really, the idea of the
ideal family — it doesn't exist. It always takes
work. There's always pain as well as the good times.
Yours is just going through a major renovation
right now."

I shook my head. "You don't understand."

"I know you've gone through some bad times,
Jes. But what about all the happy memories?"

I picked up a heavy stone, tried to skip it, but it
sunk immediately. "Those are the worst ones. The
good memories are the lies. If they were true — if
we were happy — how did we end up like this?"
Tears sprang to my eyes and I couldn't keep them
from falling, even though I was mostly mad. It was
like a faucet had turned on and I couldn't stop it. "I
hate the good memories most of all."

Amber took me in her arms. I didn't push her
away. "Okay, you're right," she said. "That is sad …
okay." She hugged me until I stopped crying.

"Don't tell her," I said.

"You should tell her yourself, Jes. She wants to
know."

"I can't. I just can't. It's like all these bits of me keep getting split up and blown all over the place. I can't keep having bits of me floating around everywhere."

She nodded and handed me a crumpled tissue from her pocket. "I remember the first time Sam went to camp," she said.

So did I. He wanted me to come with him, but I wouldn't. Mom and Dad had just split up and I was afraid to let either one of them out of my sight. I thought they would disappear off the face of the earth if I did. I even had nightmares about it. Me floating all alone in space.

"He was nervous about going," Amber continued. "And so was I. I was afraid he'd wake up in the middle of the night, and I wouldn't be there. I almost didn't let him go, but Geoff insisted.

"Well, he had the time of his life, and when he came back, the first thing he said to me was 'I didn't miss you at all.'" She smiled ruefully at the memory. I'd always wondered what a rueful smile was like when I read about it in books. I made a mental note now.

"But I just listened to him and laughed at all his stories. Then I went to my room and cried for an hour straight. I felt very sorry for myself. Geoff came in and I blubbered about how Sam didn't need me anymore. But Geoff just said it seemed to him that the only thing that was going on was that

I'd done a good job. It was my job to let him go, bit by bit. But I hadn't let him go willingly. If I could have, I'd have pitched a tent beside his cabin and stayed there for the week."

"That would have gone over big," I said.

She laughed and smacked my knee lightly. "Exactly. That's the hardest part, the letting go. But the ironic part is that that's where the freedom is. Right at the moment of letting go. And ultimately that's all we ever have, you know? Right at the moment."

"But that's the way it's supposed to be, Amber. Parents are supposed to let their kids go … not the other way around."

Amber shook her head. "It's not so much that we let go of the people we love … we need to let go of who we think they're supposed to be. That's the trick, sweetie. That's the challenge. Until you do, you'll just be clinging on … you'll never fly. So what you have to figure out is, what are you clinging to? And how are you going to let go? It takes courage, Jes."

A part of me knew what she meant, but the truth was that my mom and dad had let go of each other.

"Okay."

Amber took a deep breath. "I don't know if your mom ever told you this, but — it's still hard to say … my mother killed herself, Jes."

"I'm so sorry, Amber. I didn't know."

"No," she waved her hand. "That's not why I'm telling you. I was just thinking that when we don't tell things to our children, especially the painful things, they get this impression that we haven't lived. And I wanted you to know that I have ... lived."

"It must have been awful," I whispered.

"Worse than awful. She didn't leave a note or anything."

"Then how did you get through it?"

"Well, I decided that if I couldn't have an explanation, I could at least find meaning. When you said now that I have it made, I guess it looks like that ... like it's easy or lucky or a fluke. But honestly, Jes, that's not how it feels. It feels like I took the sadness of my mother's life and I made it mean something for me. I never take a day for granted."

I thought of all the times I'd seen Amber in her lawn chair with a book and a smile, or laughing and talking with my mom — the way she played with her kids. I'd always considered her a happy person, but I thought she was just born that way.

"Maybe it sounds arrogant. I don't know," she continued. "But my life is my accomplishment. Some women have careers or houses or kids that do it for them, but I look at my happiness and I say, 'You know what? I went looking for that.'"

"I don't know if you'll ever find an explanation

that will help you understand why your parents split, but, sweetie, if you look for the meaning, you'll find it."

"But not everything has meaning," I said. "Alberta died too soon. My mom and dad couldn't make it together. Now mom's getting married — *forever* — again. It's just so complicated."

"I know," she said. "But your mother is choosing to keep living, Jes. That takes a lot of courage."

She held my hand, and I was grateful that she didn't say anything more.

Back at the campground, Amber offered to make lunch for me, but I said I wasn't hungry. I told her I needed to go for a swim.

"All right. But stay in the swimming area," she said, sounding like a mother again.

I changed into my bathing suit and walked down to the wharf. I swam until my arms and legs were tingling with tiredness. Then I climbed up on the wharf and practiced my dives.

Dad had taught me to dive. I was scared, but I trusted him. He's a great swimmer, barely even disturbs the water when he moves.

The kneeling dives were fine because I could imagine I was tumbling. But when he said it was time to dive from a standing position, I froze.

"Bend," he had said. "Bend and fall. Let gravity do the work."

Like I even knew what gravity was.

"Gravity is the force that keeps you from floating away. It holds you to the ground," he explained.

I think he meant it to be a comforting explanation. It wasn't. Especially when the ground in question is below tons of water.

So I listened to him and I trusted gravity and I let myself fall. But I guess part of me wasn't quite so sure and my body resisted, betrayed me, landing with a magnificent "thwap." Belly flop ... good name for it.

Immediately I felt the failure sting my bare stomach, and as I popped up, I looked behind me. Dad grinned and waved. "Just keep on swimming," he said. My failure was official. I hadn't dived the way I'd seen him do a thousand times. I had flopped — belly first. The tears burned in my eyes even though the lake tried to wash them away.

For the first time, but not the last, I thought, I can't let him see me cry. But the first time is always the worst.

He apologized as soon as I climbed up on the wharf. He hugged me in those tanned arms and said, "I'm sorry, kiddo." He knew. But it didn't help. It didn't make it better, and that was worse than the belly flop.

After that I practiced by myself when I was sure no one was watching. I would wait until he was out on his boat fishing. After a few weeks I asked him to come to the wharf with me. It was an especially hot night — with the evening sand still holding the heat of the sun. Neither of us spoke, and he followed me to the end of the dock. I closed my eyes, and I dove. I knew it was a perfect dive immediately. And when I looked back, the setting sun was reflected in his eyes.

"Oh, Funny Face," was all he said.

It was a wonderful moment. But I knew, even then, that it wasn't about trusting gravity.

"Hey, Elf," Sam's voice surprised me now and I jumped.

I looked over my shoulder and was relieved to see that he was alone.

"Sorry. Didn't mean to scare you," he grinned, white teeth against his tanned skin.

"You got your braces off!" I yelped.

"Thanks for finally noticing."

"Well, I've barely seen you lately."

"Whose fault is that?" he answered, sounding defensive.

I ignored this. "They look great, your teeth I mean."

He grinned again, exaggerating this time.

I put my hand over my eyes. "Okay, okay, you're blinding me here."

He closed his mouth quickly. "Sorry about that. I'll have to remember to use my new powers wisely."

"I think I can control myself," I said.

There was an awkward moment, and I realized I'd embarrassed him.

"I didn't mean ..." he began.

"Kidding, Sam."

More awkward moments.

"We're going to the rope swing. Come with us."

There was that word again. Us. But it didn't include me anymore. I was on the outside.

"Always my favorite activity," I said.

"What's with you lately?"

"What's with me? What's with you?"

"You don't have to be like this."

"Like what?"

"Like all weird."

"Yes, I do," I said.

Sam smiled at this and it just made me madder. His smile was all perfect now. I missed the overlapping tooth in the front. And then I wondered if I did want to be more than friends with him, and the thought made me back up so that I nearly toppled off the dock. His smile widened and he reached out to take my hand, but I regained my balance without him. It took every bit of self-control I had not to charge him and push him off the dock.

"Come with us," he said.

"Oh, Sam," I began, wanting to tell him about what I'd seen in the maze. And then it was one of those stupid soap-opera moments where the character stops just before spilling the beans — "you're really my long lost twin brother" — or something equally stupid. The truth was, I stopped because I couldn't stand the thought of hurting him. I could tell he liked Angela. He was proud to be with her. And I couldn't do it.

"I'm not coming," I said.

The noise of a motor interrupted us. It was Tim's boat. Marshall was driving it. Angela and Dell were perched in the front seat, waving. Seeing Dell's face brought back the morning's events: Marshall and Angela tangled together in the cornfield.

"Suit yourself," Sam said, before turning and stepping into the boat.

I walked down the dock quickly, ignoring Dell's calls. I made it to the porch of the cabin before giving in to the urge to watch them leave. Dell's face grew smaller, but she was looking at me. I raised my hand and waved. And I felt incredibly sad. Could I ever tell her what had happened?

We had made a vow once, with bloodied fingers entwined. "Withhold nothing." We were proud of the phrase, Dell especially since she'd come up with it, but I had shared in the pride. It seemed magical. For all time we would keep nothing from each other. We were blood sisters — not so original maybe — but our blood had met at the tips of our fingers and would travel through our veins to the end of time. And with it, the truth of everything we experienced would flow between us.

The kiss between Marshall and Angela now threatened all of that. If I shared what I knew, what would happen? And I knew that even in the hours that had already passed, I had withheld. The magic had been broken.

16

Dad dropped me off at the house on Sunday afternoon. There was a note from Mom on the kitchen table saying that she and Cal would be home at seven o'clock. There was a P.S.: "Mrs. K wants to know if you can baby-sit. Call her if you get home in time."

Relieved, I phoned Mrs. Kennedy and said I'd be glad to come over.

Lucy met me in the driveway. As soon as her mom left, she pulled me into the backyard. As I pushed her on the swing, I noticed she was less talkative than usual.

"How's it going, Lucille?" I asked with a big push. Her little legs hung limply from the swing. She didn't answer. "Hey, how about a little pumping there?"

But she still didn't say anything. I moved to the front, took hold of the chains and brought the swing to a halt. She jumped off and climbed into my lap.

"I hate Dickie Rathbone," she said against my chest.

"I thought he was your best friend."

"He is my worst friend. I hate him," she scowled.

"Since when?"

"Since yesterday."

"What happened?"

"He is so stupid. Boys are stupid."

"Okay, what did he do?"

"I just asked him what his normal blinking speed was, and he said that was dumb."

"Normal blinking speed?" I asked gently.

She turned her little face up to mine. "Yeah, like this." She fluttered her curly lashes twice. "That's a normal blinking speed for me. But sometimes people go like this." Now she blinked rapidly, like something was in her eyes. "Or like this." She demonstrated again in slow motion. I tried not to smile.

"Well, it seems like a good question."

"Yeah!" she agreed emphatically. "But he said it was dumb."

"Maybe he was just in a bad mood."

"No." She shook her head so that her pigtails flapped across her face. "It was because his friends were there. Stupid Jerome and Stupid Cameron."

I coughed to cover up my smile, but she didn't notice.

"They said only girls say stuff like that."

I understood immediately. But how could I explain it to her?

I helped her up onto the swing again and pushed. "You know, sometimes boys act differently around their friends — their guy friends, I mean."

"How come?" Her little legs moved back and forth slightly.

"Because sometimes they get teased for having a friend who's a girl."

"How come?"

I pushed a little harder and tried to come up with a good answer. Any answer.

"Oh, I don't know. Maybe his friends were saying that you're his girlfriend."

"Yuck!" she said loudly. Now her legs pumped furiously, propelling her higher. I stood back and watched. "I hate Dickie Rathbone," she yelled.

"No, you don't," I said, but she didn't hear me.

I watched as Lucy expended all her energy on pumping the swing higher and higher. She didn't even know that she was doing it on her own for the very first time. She had no clue how much power she had. Then suddenly she seemed to realize how high she'd gone, and she froze. She looked down at me, terrified.

"Don't let go," I yelled.

"Jes," she screamed as she let go.

But I was there, behind her, and I managed to break her fall as she slipped out of the seat. It wasn't the most comfortable landing in the world, but it only knocked the breath out of me and she was fine. Except that she was crying. The tears flowed from her like a dam had burst. I held on.

"It'll be okay, Lucy."

"He hates me." The words came out in gasps. We weren't talking about Dickie anymore, but I didn't think she knew that. It was just heartbreaking.

"I'm here," is all I said, and eventually she calmed down.

I read her a dozen stories that night. After she'd fallen asleep I sat beside her, stroking her hair.

When Mrs. Kennedy came home, she found me in Lucy's room. I looked up as she entered and I thought, I don't care what your story is.

I walked out into the hallway and she followed me. I could feel the anger rising up, so I waited until we'd moved into the living room.

She held out money to me. I shook my head and she pushed it toward me. I was shaking, but my voice was calm.

"I don't want the money."

"What's wrong, Jessica? Did something happen to the girl?"

I shook my head. "She's fine. No, that's not true."

"Is she hurt?" A look of concern actually crossed her face.

"Do you have any idea how much Lucy loves

you?" Now my voice was shaking.

"She's my daughter," she said, drawing herself up, trying to look like the adult.

"Don't ever call her 'the girl' again. Please," I said. And I left the house.

Mom's door was closed when I got home. From the thin line of light beneath, I figured she was awake, but I didn't go in. I tiptoed past to my own room. It was dark, and for a second I thought Angela might be asleep. But her lamp clicked on as soon as I walked in. Great. The last thing I needed right now was a conversation with her.

"Hey," she said.

"Hi." I dropped my pack on the bed. "You know, I just realized I'm starving. I'm gonna go make myself a sandwich."

"I'll come with you."

Terrific.

I made myself a peanut butter and banana sandwich.

Angela looked uneasy. "You're going to actually eat that?"

"It tastes better than it looks," I defended my ugly snack.

"Hopefully. Listen, Jes, I've been meaning to talk to you about something."

Okay. I took a bite and chewed. I waited for the apology. Although, really, she owed it to Sam and Dell, not me.

"What do you think about having a shower for your mom next week? The wedding is only two weeks away, you know."

I chewed quickly and swallowed the bite with a swish of milk.

"That's what you wanted to talk about?"

"What else is there?" She looked straight at me.

I sputtered. "How about what happened in the cornfield yesterday? What I saw?"

Her eyes narrowed into cat's eyes. "What do you think you saw?"

"Think I saw? You were kissing Dell's boyfriend."

"He was kissing me! He just grabbed me. He totally caught me off guard."

I shook my head. "You didn't look off guard."

"How long were you there?"

What did that have to do with anything? "Not long. It was an uncomfortable moment," I said, looking straight into her eyes. She looked straight back so I could see that she had little flecks of gold in her eyes. I wondered what her normal blinking speed was.

Then she sat down as though she was tired. "I did push him away. You didn't see that, I guess. I don't expect you to believe me."

"I didn't say I didn't believe you."

"Do you believe me?"

I weighed the evidence quickly. It was true I'd only seen them briefly. But it was also true that I'd seen her steal a pair of earrings ... Was someone's boyfriend all that different? But then it was also true that I was jealous of her. I couldn't even pretend it wasn't the case. And jealousy was a big, fat, green blob that made it difficult to see around. I sighed.

"I guess so."

"No, you don't," she said, looking away. "It's okay, though. I'm used to it."

"What do you mean?"

"Nothing. I'm just used to it, that's all. I don't have tons of friends, okay?"

"Why not?"

"You wouldn't understand. You have Dell and Sam, and they think you're great."

"So why don't you have friends?" I pushed.

She shook her head. "You're going to think I'm completely stuck-up ... and I know it sounds lame, but sometimes I think ... how I look? It just puts people off or something."

She blushed when she said this. It did sound really stuck-up, but it was also completely true. I felt sluglike and I squirmed.

"I guess I could see that happening," I said, forcing the ugly, green blob into the corner, where it taunted me. It wasn't leaving the room completely.

"So you do believe me?"

I didn't answer right away. What was going through my head was that sometimes a person just chooses to believe something because there's no way of knowing for sure. It's like you have two roads ahead of you and they're both, you know, paved. I mean, if one of them was gravel or something or heading toward a sheer cliff, then you'd know to take the other one. But that wasn't the case here. Argh! My mother's voice had made its way into my head and it made me shudder. So then I did answer, and I told her I believed her. I wasn't sure that it was true, only that it was a choice I was making. "Yeah, I do," I repeated.

A bright grin split her face and she looked genuinely happy. "So, what do I do? Do I tell Dell?"

The shift was heady. I'd gone from accuser to confidante. This self-assured, beautiful giant wanted my advice. But my confidence was temporary. I hated the thought of lying to Dell, and I hated the thought of hurting her.

"I don't know."

"Well," Angela sounded brisk, "it's been my experience that a snake will make himself known soon enough. I say we keep it quiet — he'll show his true colors eventually."

It made sense. And it meant not having to hurt Dell, so I nodded. But it was one of those choices again … only, deep down, I had a bad feeling about this one.

"I like Sam, you know. I really do, Jes."

My heart did a little ka-thump and I took a bite

of my sandwich. The banana was a little slimy, I thought, forcing it down.

"He's really nice," she added.

Nice. What a stupid word to describe Sam. He was so much more than that.

"Have you seen his pictures?" I asked, staring at the peanut butter oozing out the sides of my sandwich. What was I thinking? It really was a gross snack.

"Pictures?"

Inexplicably my mood lifted. So he hadn't shown her.

"He's an amazing photographer. It's how he looks at the world. One moment at a time," I said carefully. "He showed me this picture once, of his brothers, Henry and Danny. It was Henry's birthday and he was opening one of his gifts. Danny was just watching." Angela stood there with her head slightly forward as though waiting for something exciting. I sped my words up. "Anyway, Sam said he thought he was taking a shot of Henry, but when he got the picture back and he saw Danny with his hands over his face like this" — I did a visual demonstration of fingers spread across my face, trying not to get peanut butter on myself — "he realized that the real picture was of Danny. Danny was so excited and nervous about the gift he was giving to Henry and, well, that's what Sam said, that he hadn't known that that was where the real picture, the real story was." My voice flickered away because I knew I'd lost my audience.

Angela looked at me with her bright green eyes. "I wonder if he could take some head shots for me."

There really was nothing I could say to this, so Angela went up to bed while I garburated the rest of my sandwich. My appetite was completely gone. As I was putting my dishes into the dishwasher, I thought about our conversation and wished there had been someone there with a camera to snap away. What would the real picture have showed?

Then Mom's face appeared in the doorway.

"Hey, Mom."

She opened the fridge door. "Want some orange juice?"

"No, thanks."

She poured herself a glass, then sat down. "How was your weekend? Was the maze as amazing as ever?" She took a sip of juice.

"It was pretty amazing."

"Good. Did Angela mention the shower? Because you don't have to do it. Really. I'm hardly a blushing bride and I don't need —"

"I'll do it," I said.

"Are you sure?"

I nodded as I reached for a dishcloth to wipe up my crumbs.

"Jes?"

"Yeah?"

"I know I've been busy with the wedding and you haven't been around much, but we need to talk about the other day — about what I told you."

"No, we don't," I said, holding on to the door handle, looking down at the floor.

She rose from the table, but didn't seem to know where to go from there. "I should have told you a long time ago, I suppose."

"No, you shouldn't have, Mom," I said. "You should never, ever have told me." And I left the room.

The next day, things were pretty chilly around the house. It was like Mom decided to put me on her "wait until after the wedding" list of things to do. I decided to be part of Wedding Storm only when I had to.

"Do you want to come with us to buy decorations, Jes?" Angela asked after breakfast. "Dell's coming. She's got some great ideas."

"Whatever you pick out will be fine."

I was weeding in the backyard when Dell came over.

"Hey, you coming to the mall with us?" she asked.

I pretended to faint, falling against the rock wall. "I get weak even thinking about it."

She smiled and said in a low, narrator's voice.

"Her knees turned gelatinous at the very thought of … dum, dum, dum … entering the mall."

"Gelatinous. Good word, Dell."

Her smile faded, and she shrugged.

Suddenly I was mad at what Marshall was doing to her, what he was taking from her. He was like a worm eating his way into her soul. Without thinking, I ripped off my gardening gloves and sat her down on the wooden bench.

"What's with you?" But she made no move to get up. Her eyes were trusting.

"The other day, at the cornfield? Oh, Dell, I should have told you right away."

"Told me what?"

"I saw Marshall and Angela together."

"So?"

"Kissing. In the maze, I saw them. Kissing … each other." I added the last part because Dell was looking at me strangely, as though she hadn't understood.

She got up from the bench slowly.

"I'm sorry, Dell. She said he just grabbed her …" Already I was in hot water. How much did I say now? Why had I even started this? "I just hated that you didn't know. You should know who he is." I could see my mom trying to say the same exact thing last night in the kitchen, and I pushed the thought away. "I'm so sorry, Dell."

She didn't say anything. She stood there curling one long strand of hair around her finger like it was really important.

"You don't have to be jealous of Marshall," she said quietly.

"You don't believe me?" I squeaked. I never would have anticipated this reaction. Not in a million years. She just didn't want this to be true.

"I don't know what to believe. You've changed, Jes."

"I've changed! What about you? I don't even know who you are anymore when you're with Marshall. And now he's got you doubting your-self ..." And not believing me, I could have added, but didn't.

She shook her long campfire curls at me. "You want everything to stay the same, Jes, until you're ready for it to change. But you can't do that. You can't expect the whole world to stand still until you're ready."

Some of what she was saying made ugly sense to me, but it was silhouetted against the backdrop of a lie. And I hadn't lied. I had seen what I had seen.

"Angela was worried that you might be jealous of Marshall and me ... of her and Sam. But, Jes, I think I might love him. Don't make me choose between you."

My head was spinning, like the whole world had broken free from gravity and was whirling off into space.

I took a deep breath. "Maybe I am a little jealous of Angela and Sam ... of Angela and you." Admitting this felt like a stone being lifted off my chest and then dropped right back down again. "But I am not lying to you, Dell. Honest."

As far back as Dell and I went, the promise of "honest" went with us. It was our solemn vow that whatever followed was complete truth. We would never question each other once that word was spoken, and we had never said it lightly.

But she didn't say anything.

Then Angela came out of the house. As Dell passed her, she asked, "What's wrong?" But Dell kept moving, disappearing into the house.

"You should have left it alone," Angela said. And she followed Dell into the house.

I was numb down to my toes. Somehow I had turned into the bad guy. And I knew I couldn't stay.

17

I sat at the very back of the bus, placing my knapsack beside me so no one would sit there. I'd made this trip alone a few times when Dad would stay up at the cabin for a month in the summer and I'd join him for the weekends. I had a knack for attracting grandmas who loved to show me pictures of their grandchildren. Normally I didn't mind — they usually had food they liked to share. But today I wanted to be alone.

I watched the trees rush past the smudged window, decorated by some kid's peanut butter hands. I left a note saying I'd gone to Dad's. I figured I had a day, maybe two, before my mother caught on.

I had a plan: a couple days of swimming, fishing and star spinning. I didn't want to see anybody or talk to anybody. All I wanted to hear and taste and feel was Mara. She was the only real thing left.

I waved to the bus driver as he pulled away, leaving me in a cloud of diesel fumes. I carefully avoided the Schmidts' cabin, even though I was pretty sure they weren't up here this week.

The first thing I did was swim until I ached. Then I fished and caught nothing except an ugly dogfish. I threw it back and decided on hot dogs for dinner or, rather, wieners, since the buns in the cupboard had gone green.

The phone rang. I ignored it.

I built a fire in the pit and roasted three wieners and a cob of corn and ate as I watched the sunset — the transition of sky from deep azure to filmy gray, then charcoal, and then the night was black. The moon was a sliver, a crescent moon. It was my favorite kind. Even though Sam liked to call it "Grandpa's Toenail." I liked it because you could see it two ways. At first glance, it was a delicate, fragile wisp of pure light; but if you kept looking, you could make out the shadow of the entire orb behind, completing it, and you knew that the sun's light was still there, illuminating part of the whole. And then, in a sleight of hand, all you could see was the golden sliver again. It took faith, it seemed, to imagine the full moon, but you knew it was there in the shadows.

But tonight my eyes kept focusing on the illuminated rim, and I couldn't see the whole. It was as though I didn't even believe it was there anymore. All that existed was what you could see. And it made me sad.

I doused the fire and stood with my arms raised
to the stars. I spun around and tried to feel the way
I used to, when I would become part of the liquid
starshine, when the earth would fall away and I
would float inside the stream of light. But I
couldn't feel anything. I was just standing on a
beach with my feet in the chilly, damp sand and my
arms stuck straight up in the air like an idiot. The
magic was gone.

I couldn't sleep that night. The shadows inside the
cabin were new to me and they danced eerily on
the walls of my bedroom. Finally I took my
sleeping bag outside and wrapped myself in it,
lying down on the recliner on the porch. A foreign
smell came off the tar-black water. It was a deep
night smell.

The moon was nowhere to be seen now, and
even the starlight seemed swathed in inkiness. I'd
never seen Mara so dark, never thought she was
capable of it. I pulled the sleeping bag closer
around me. The boats moored at the dock seemed
perched on top as if in a painting, stuck forever,
along with the swimming wharf and the buoys out
beyond. The lack of movement frightened me.

In all the years I'd been coming here, I'd always
seen Mara as welcoming, like an old friend. But not
tonight. I shivered again. Nothing could make me
step into that water. If I did, I was sure I would be

pulled under. The only light came from the trucks driving on the highway parallel to the lake, but it didn't pierce the flatness, only skated across it, and then it was black again.

I closed my eyes and tried to pretend it was all a terrible nightmare.

When I woke up, my nose was freezing and there were clouds resting on the tops of the surrounding mountains. They were lit bright orange from beneath, soft against a violet sky. The sun was still far behind the mountain, but there was enough light to awaken the lake. I could hear the fish move, and see an occasional ripple as they jumped to catch an early breakfast. The wind was sending a trickle of steady waves to beat on the shore. The dark night's spell had been broken.

But even as I dragged my sleeping bag back inside the cabin for more sleep, something had changed. I had seen Mara as I was never meant to see her, and pretending wouldn't take the knowing away.

I woke up later to see Leonard's face peeking in through the window. I kind of figured they might get to him. I let him in.

"You coming fishing?" he asked.

"Yup."

We didn't speak again until we were in the middle of the lake. The morning mist rose around us and seagulls followed — hopeful and loud.

"I phoned your mom while you were getting ready. Told her you were here," Leonard said as he cast his line.

"Was she mad?"

He shrugged his lean shoulders. "I expect."

"Ooh. But her voice didn't sound like it?" I winced. "That's, like, third-degree mad."

His head tilted a fraction. "She loves you," he said simply.

"Do you miss her?" I asked.

He nodded. "Do you?"

I turned my attention to my tangled line and when I'd finally succeeded in undoing the knots, I cast. The line arched through the air with a pleasant "zing," landing a good ways from the boat.

"Nice cast, Jes."

"I miss who she was. And I miss who we were together," I said. "Why does everything have to change?" I felt a tug at the end of my line and I wound the reel up quickly, but it was empty except for a piece of snagged weed.

Eventually I gave up fishing and leaned back against one of the life jackets, pulling my cap down to shade my face.

"Are you up for a story?" he asked.

I nodded my head and felt my cap bump up and down on my nose.

"You know who the Buddha was?"

"Some rich guy's son who threw it all away to

search for the light," I said, scanning my brain for more information that Leonard had passed along over the years. He knew lots of different stories, and sometimes I got them muddled up. "And suffering. He was into suffering."

Leonard smiled at this. "Well, not 'into suffering' exactly, but he felt it was part of every life — our common lot — and not shameful." He cast his line out into the water. "And on the night of the Buddha's enlightenment, after he had vowed to awaken, he was attacked by the armies of Mara ..."

"For real?" I interrupted, peeking up under my cap. "Mara?"

"Mara was the god of illusion and evil," he said, letting out his line slowly. "The Buddha was seated under the Bodhi Tree when Mara came upon him, tempting him with greed and fear and doubt and even pleasure. But the Buddha was able to resist him — even able to overcome the anger unleashed, because he saw Mara with a heart of compassion. And so Mara left, defeated, but only temporarily. Many times afterward Mara returned to fight or to tempt or to undermine the Buddha, but each time, in every different story, the Buddha recognized Mara and so was not caught by temptation. 'Is that you again, Mara?' the Buddha would ask, and every time Mara would slip away because he had been recognized."

I listened to the story, the sound of his words as

they rose and fell like the sound of the water against the weathered wood of the boat. The rhythm of the lake seemed to punctuate his sentences, but it wasn't a comforting feeling, and the wind was blowing now, a little colder, it felt, although the sky was clear. Whitecaps were rising around us, churned up by the wind. I didn't understand the story, but I knew I didn't like it. I dipped my hand into the water and it still felt warm. "It doesn't feel like an illusion," I mumbled.

"It never does at the time. The point of the story, I think, is that we have to recognize the illusion and ask ourselves, what is the truth inside of it? And you can only recognize it with a heart of compassion."

Suddenly, I was furious. "Why did you tell me that horrible story? What if I can't ever look at Mara the same now? What if you've ruined it? What if everything is ruined?"

He seemed surprised by my outburst and reached out to touch my foot, but I pulled it away.

"Seeing something as it truly is can't ruin it, Jes. It can only expose what's really there."

But I couldn't answer. I couldn't even look at Leonard. What if I didn't want what's really there? What if I'd rather have the illusion, the bright, shining lake instead of a dark, moody, suffering monster?

Stupid, stupid Leonard. I wouldn't look at him. Instead I watched the churning waves as he turned the boat toward home. As soon as the dock came into view, I could see my father standing there, his red flannel shirt blowing in the breeze.

He helped us with the boat, and I got out quickly. I didn't want to talk to him. From the way he was standing there, looking at me, I knew Mom had told him. He knew that I knew, and he couldn't look me in the eyes.

I waited as he said good-bye to Leonard and then he approached me. His hug felt weird — empty.

"We were pretty worried about you, Funny Face."

"Don't call me that."

"Oh. Guess it's not true anymore, is it? Remember when you lost your two front teeth. That's when I started to … um …" he trailed off.

"Did you come to take me home, Dad? Because I'd really like to stay — just until the wedding. I can't be around there. I'm in the way."

"Your mom was upset, Jes. Really worried. You're not in her way —"

"You don't know. How could you? I am in the way. All she cares about is that ridiculous wedding and that happily-ever-after-till-death-do-you-part crap!"

"Don't talk about your mother that way."

"You don't get to tell me how to talk about my mother anymore," I said, walking to the edge of the wharf.

"You shouldn't be angry with her. You should be angry with me. I should have explained it to you a long time ago. I just couldn't stand the thought of the look on your face." His eyes met mine then, and I knew it was all true. I mean, I guess I knew it before. But now I felt it — right down to my bones.

"Be angry with me, Jes. Not with your mom."

"I can't be angry with you, Dad." I twisted my cap in my hands, then put it back on my head. "I can't. You're too sad all the time. You read your sad books, you live in a sad house. You do sad little jobs ... you eat sad food." I backed away from him. "I can't —" Tears were gathering. In his eyes, too.

"Jes, come back. Let's talk about this."

"It won't change anything." As soon as my foot hit the sand of the shore, I ran to the woods. When I reached the edge and looked back, he was still standing there. He looked small to me. For the first time in my life, he seemed small.

I ran most of the way to the rope swing. I climbed to the top of the cliff. There were dark clouds gathering above the hills. A storm was coming. I could smell the rawness of the water. Then I noticed the Schmidt boat motoring its way across the lake in a direct line to the swing. I wondered if Dad had borrowed it, but then I saw that Sam was driving.

I ducked behind the trees until I was sure he was past. If I saw him, I would tell him ... everything.

Dad, Angela, Marshall … everything. It would all come spilling out and I couldn't risk it. I couldn't risk losing him, too. I thought of Leonard's stupid story again. What if love itself was an illusion?

When the motor was a faint put-put in the distance, I came to the cliff's edge. I took off the tracksuit I was wearing over my bathing suit and grabbed the rope. It felt rough and dry in my hands and I clutched it for a long time. The wind had changed and I knew the rain wasn't far behind.

I closed my eyes and tried to make my feet push away from the ground, but at the last second, I opened them and saw the water swirling below me in a jagged froth. I swerved dizzily and would have fallen except for a sudden gust of wind that helped me regain my balance. I fell against a log, grasping anything solid — the dirt, a rock … anything that would hold me.

Tears fell down my face. I wasn't hurt or anything. And I didn't think I was crying about the other stuff. I'd just wanted to jump. On my own. It would have meant something.

Sitting here in the dirt, afraid and alone — that meant something, too.

The rain hit as we drove home later that afternoon. Mom had nixed the idea of my staying at the cabin until the wedding. I didn't bother to argue.

Dad tried to make conversation.

"Maybe, after the wedding, you and I can take off for a week or so before school starts?"

"Sure, maybe," I answered.

"Or we could just go to the lake."

"Okay."

We drove through the outskirts of town and turned down our street. In the driveway, he said to me, staring at the steering wheel, "It was the biggest mistake I've ever made."

I grabbed my pack and pulled the car door open. "No kidding." I looked at him only for a second, and I wondered if I'd ever really known him. Maybe I'd just made him up so he'd be the dad I remembered. I ran up the stairs and slammed the door behind me.

18

When I walked in the front door, Mom had a harried look about her.

Cal was sitting on the leather chair — the reading chair — where my dad's ghost had remained long after he had left. Mom had told him he should take the chair in the settlement — all the grooves and cracks had been worn in by him — but he had left it, and I'd always been grateful. Now I wished he'd taken it, so I could have been spared seeing another man sitting in it as though he belonged.

Suddenly every single thing my parents had done in the last five years seemed selfish to me. They'd only been thinking about themselves. Everything else was a lie, a cover-up. An illusion, like Leonard's terrible story.

I must have stood there for a while, because finally Mom approached, clearing her throat. "Jessica, you had us pretty worried."

Us. She was an "us" without me or my dad. We

could be on the other side of the world and she would still be an "us."

Cal got up clumsily from the chair, almost tripping on the ottoman. "I'll leave you two alone."

Mom held out an arm. "No. Stay."

"Heel," I muttered, as Cal hovered between sitting and standing. I almost pitied his awkwardness.

"Jessica, that was uncalled for," Mom barked.

I ignored her. "My mom has control issues, Cal. You'd better get used to it."

My mother's face turned an unattractive purple and I felt a twinge of nervousness. But also a new and unfamiliar sensation — something like power. I wasn't sure.

"Elli, it's okay. I'll be in the kitchen." And he left.

I could tell she was taking a couple of deep breaths, which gave me time to wander over to the chair he had vacated and slouch into it. The leather squeaked and its aroma settled around me.

"You owe him an apology," she finally said.

"I don't owe him anything."

She sat across from me and shook her head hard like it was an Etch A Sketch and she wanted to create a new picture. "Let's start again." She took another deep breath, calming herself. It had the opposite effect on me, because she was morphing into Therapist Mom. I knew what came next.

"Help me to understand," she began, but I muttered the words at the exact same time because I'd heard them so often. She went purple again.

"What do you want?" she said finally. Her voice was hoarse, as though she was choking on the words.

I just shook my head.

"No, really, Jes. What do you want me to do?" Now she was almost pleading.

A few days ago, I would have said I wanted things to be the way they were, like that day in the playhouse with my mom and dad's laughter surrounding me and Alberta still alive inside her. Or those months when we'd had her with us. I could remember watching Mom nurse her, mesmerized by a process I had forgotten. Or Dad's goofy songs he'd make up to put Alberta to sleep at night. He said he sang the same songs to me. But now I knew they were all illusions, flickering and sputtering. I didn't know what was real anymore. Maybe I had made up all the happy memories.

"Nothing," I finally said.

"Do you want me to cancel the wedding?"

"Would you?" I countered quickly.

"It wouldn't solve anything," she said sadly. "Did you think your father and I would get back together one day?"

"Of course ..." The words dangled like a fish line. I was planning to say, "Of course not." That was in my head. But it wasn't in my heart, and I couldn't finish the sentence. It stayed there, hovering in the air between us.

For the first time ever in her life, I'd bet, she had no words.

As I walked down the hallway, I caught my reflection in the hall mirror. But it was more like one of those fun house distorted reflections. I looked squat and shapeless, an indistinct blob … nondescript. I always thought that was a stupid word when I came across it in books. Nondescript. How could something or someone be so plain that you couldn't find one word to describe them? It was the ultimate insult, when you thought about it. What did she look like? Shrug. Nondescript.

I stepped closer to the mirror, searching for the one word that could describe me. I got close enough so that I could peer right into those eyes that peered back at me. But it was as though I looked at no one. Or rather, no one looked back. No one was home.

When I walked into my room, the contrast was startling. Angela looked perfectly at home. I had been replaced by the ideal daughter. She looked the part, for sure. Plus, she did dishes and probably windows as well.

She'd been cleaning again. No matter how much I had tried to continue occupying my dwindling space — strewn socks, discarded sweatshirts, half-opened books — she managed to make it look as though I'd never existed. She was the Zamboni of roommates.

Angela looked up from her bed, where she was wrapped in a blanket — mine — and reading a magazine. She looked concerned.

"Hey," she said. She jumped up from the bed and hugged me. "I was so worried! Your mom was freaking out ... so was Cal."

"I'm sorry," I muttered, brushing past her. I dumped my stuff out on my bed. Sand and grit poured out. I'd packed in a hurry. A musty lake smell permeated the crisp, Lysol-scented air. "I just needed to get away."

"Because of your conversation with Dell? I talked to her, explained everything. I told her you were just trying to protect her."

Angela had explained me to my best friend? Indignation rose up in my chest. I forced it down.

I shook my clothes out for something to do, and I thought I heard an intake of breath from Angela.

"I just vacuumed," she said.

"Uh-huh," I continued to shake my clothes out. Maybe next time I'd bring a bucket of sand and spread it around my bed ... see how that went over.

I was considering the possibility that I was being childish when Cal knocked on the door and said there was a phone call for Angela. He entered the room with the cordless phone. "It's your mother," he said.

Angela took the phone from him and left the room, leaving me with Cal.

"I'm glad you're okay," he said. "You should get some rest." And then he left the room.

I plunked down on my bed and felt the uncomfortable grittiness of the sand beneath my feet. Who cared. It was my room, wasn't it? Nobody asked her to take on maid duties. The wedding was only a couple of weeks away. Angela would be leaving soon after. Things wouldn't be the same, but at least I'd have my space back. Maybe I'd get one of those little hot-plate deals and start cooking my meals in here. I could haul in some soil and grow my own vegetables ... maybe get a couple of chickens.

I was constructing a little dream-room, complete with a ladder outside my window, when Angela returned. She looked flushed, uncharacteristically disturbed. I wondered what could have caused this unkempt state. Her hair was actually messy in an unattractive way.

"What's up?"

She stood in the middle of the room, like she didn't know where to put herself.

"Let's go shopping," she said curtly.

"I think I'm under house arrest."

"We'll tell them we're going wedding-present shopping. I have to get out of here."

Shopping was the last thing I wanted to do, but waiting in here for mom's inevitable "follow-up" conversation didn't seem like a whole lot of fun either.

"Okay," I said, and Angela looked grateful.

She talked them into it. I stood in the background and watched, impressed by the way she handled them. She looked completely composed, as though nothing was the matter.

"Don't you want to talk about the conversation with your mother?" Cal asked, his normally normal face tight with concern.

Angela shook her head and smiled brightly. "Later."

"Do you want me to drive you?" Mom asked.

"We'll take the bus," Angela answered for me.

We left with the promise that we would be back before dark.

A bus was pulling up to the stop when we rounded the corner and we ran to catch it. As we boarded, everyone including very small children turned to look at Angela as we made our way to our seats. During that short trip, she received two marriage proposals and one slightly less honorable offer. She seemed oblivious to the attention, and when she sat down she stared straight in front of her.

"I have to hand it to you," I said. "You have a way with parents."

Angela continued looking straight ahead and gave what Dell would call a mirthless laugh.

"What?" I asked, but Angela remained silent.

I watched the trees and telephone poles whip by as the bus cruised along the busy street, lurching up and down potholes like a humpback whale.

"So what did your mom have to say?" I asked, making conversation.

Angela remained silent. I looked away from the street, sideways, at her face. Her jaw was clenched, the muscles on the side of her face were twitching.

"I used to play soccer," she said.

"Okay," I nodded. Not exactly what I asked, but whatever.

"I was pretty good," she said, looking straight ahead. "It was the final game of the season and my mom promised she'd come. I was, I don't know ... twelve, I guess?" She gave a shrug. "I was playing center forward and it was a big game. We had a shot at the state finals. I didn't really think she'd come — she hadn't been to a game all season — so I didn't even look at the stands to see if she'd arrived, because I wanted to stay up for the game, you know?"

I nodded, even though Angela wasn't looking at me.

"But just before we started, I couldn't resist, so I looked up and she was there. She was wearing one of her big hats and sunglasses, but she was there. I was awesome, Jes. I scored two goals before the half and another one after. We won the game. When all the excitement died down, I looked for her again and she was standing right behind me. I couldn't wait for her to tell me that I'd played well ... done a good job." Angela tugged at her hair. "You know what she said?" Now she looked at me. I shrugged.

"She said, 'I'm sorry I didn't make it to the game. The audition ran long, but I think I got the part. Let's go celebrate!'"

"She was lying?" I asked stupidly.

Angela shook her head. She looked tired. "Nope. She wasn't even at the game. The lady in the hat didn't look a thing like her, not really. But I told myself that she was my mom. I made her up, like I'd always made her up. She doesn't even exist, my mom."

I was confused.

"Haven't you ever done that? Wanted somebody to be a certain way so bad that you pretend that they are?"

I found myself nodding.

"Well, never again. Not for me. Not anymore."

"You must have felt terrible, though."

She shook her head. "Nope. You just have to be

stronger than the hurt. I've built up an immunity to her."

"So, what did she want ... before, on the phone?"

"She's landed some dumb-ass part on a soap opera ... her big break ... she thinks I should stay here." Angela's words faded, turned into background noise ... something about how ridiculous soap operas were ... but all I heard was "She thinks I should stay here."

Well, here was a perfectly horrifying thought. My brain refused to function. Angela here. Forever. That's as far as I could go.

When the bus stopped at the mall, we got out of our seats and into the narrow corridor. "You don't want me to stay, do you?"

"I — er, I didn't say that." A man jostled me with his elbow and I almost lost my balance. I didn't hear Angela's response.

I followed her into the mall, and we walked aimlessly for what seemed like a long time. My feet started to drag, and I realized that in the last few days I'd had very little sleep. "I'm really bagged," I said, whining a little.

"Let me take your knapsack," Angela said, barely breaking stride. I handed it to her as I followed her into the brightly-lit department store. It felt like every florescent bulb was pulsing its way into my brain. I knew I should say something to her about the whole staying-on thing, but what could I say ...

that I'd already planned to turn her side of the room into a chicken run? That my plans for organic farming didn't include her? That I was horrified at the thought?

We walked farther and finally I stopped, leaning against a faux marble pillar. "Must ... have ... water. You go ahead ... save yourself."

She looked at me without any expression. "I'll go scout things out. You wait here."

I nodded, slumping onto a bench. I watched her wind her way through the maze of glittering displays until she was gone.

Within moments I had worked my magic, and an old lady had parked her considerable self beside me and was brandishing pictures of her great-grandchildren.

"The little one ... that's Thomas, and that's Gerald, his older brother, screwing up his face — the minx."

"Tom and Gerry?" I clarified. "For real?"

She looked puzzled at first, but then it sunk in and she started to laugh with a "ho ho ho" like Santa Claus. I was laughing as well, when I saw Angela striding toward us, a better-looking version of the witch/neighbor from *The Wizard of Oz*.

"Any luck?" I asked.

"This place sucks. Let's go."

I saw the old lady wince at Angela's choice of words. I started to say something ... I was going to tell her to say hi to Tom and Gerry for me, but Angela had grabbed my arm and was pulling me with her.

"What's the rush?" I asked, retrieving my arm with a yank. She thrust my knapsack at me. I took it and put it on.

As we walked out of the store, the alarm rang at the exact moment the bells were going off in my head. Perfect timing.

19

They put us in separate offices. I felt like a criminal, even though I hadn't done anything wrong. Mr. Something Unpronounceable had a look of disgust on his face that might have been his permanent expression, as he lectured me on the perils of shoplifting. I waited patiently for a break in his well-rehearsed tirade.

"But I didn't lift anything," I objected.

His face screwed up as though he'd bitten into a brussels sprout. "Then how did the necklace make its way into your knapsack? Perhaps it walked?"

I was about to suggest in my most sarcastic voice that sarcasm never accomplished anything, when the phone rang.

Mr. Sneer picked up the receiver and spoke a couple of terse words. "Send her in."

There is an unwritten rule among teenagers that goes something like this: She who runs away from home should avoid troublesome activities for a fortnight hence. Translation: Always leave two weeks between screwups. I hadn't gone twenty-four hours.

Mom shot me a very un-therapistlike look before turning to Mr. Ruptured Spleen with her professional smile and introducing herself.

We went over the whole scenario. I repeated that I had taken nothing. I had never stolen anything in my life. I wasn't a liar. But they seemed less interested in my protests than in how the necklace might have made its way into my knapsack. It was so ridiculously obvious, but I wasn't going to be the one to hand Angela over. I could still see the look in her eyes when she said, "You don't want me to stay, do you?" And that soccer story. Uh-uh. It wasn't going to be me.

Finally Mr. Grimace said, "Why don't you wait outside?"

I spent the next ten minutes avoiding eye contact with the receptionist. Every few minutes she would look up and I'd hear, "Tsk, tsk." I could feel the disapproval, but I kept my head buried in a magazine, pretending to read an article about hair removal. Fascinating stuff, really.

The door opened and they came out. Mom said she would take care of setting up the times (that didn't sound good) and thanked him for not calling the police.

In the car, Mom's hands fluttered around the

ignition as though she'd forgotten the concept. Finally she stuck a key in and we drove out onto the street.

"Where's Angela?" I asked in a very tiny voice that didn't sound at all like me.

"She's with Cal. He'll take her home. Listen, Jes. This isn't over. The manager has agreed not to press charges if you and Angela do some community service. I told him I would set it up."

"But I didn't do anything! I sat in the store and looked at pictures of somebody's grandkids. Somebody's great-grandkids!" I added, as though this would make the difference. "Why didn't you tell him that I was telling the truth ... that I'm not a liar?"

With a very un-mom like move, she swerved out of traffic and came to an abrupt stop at the side of the street. She slammed the car into park and gave me a long, hard look. "I beg your pardon?"

I shrunk two sizes with that look. Okay, you write one slightly false note, run away from home for a couple of days, and you're branded for life. "So what did you tell him?"

Another long look. "I said that under no circumstances would you ever steal a pearl necklace. A pair of running shoes, maybe; a pearl necklace, never."

I thought this over.

"So, your entire defense was my bad taste?"

She shook her head and her face crinkled up. For a minute I thought she was going to cry or yell, but then she laughed. It was sort of a frustrated laugh, but it made me feel a whole lot better and I laughed with her. It was like a window opened, just a small one, but enough to let a little light in ... a bit of fresh air.

We sat and laughed until tears came to our eyes, and one of the reasons it felt so good was that she was just my mom again.

At the house, we walked toward the front door. Mom stopped me before we entered.

"I know you're protecting Angela, sweetie. I'm not sure exactly why — just be careful, okay?"

"Careful of what?"

"People are not always who they seem to be."

This was so obvious that I had to stop myself from saying, "Duh." But then it hit me. Maybe, just maybe, my mother understood Angela more than she had let on. And as we opened the front door, this thought dumbfounded me.

Angela was sitting on the couch with Cal beside her. When we came in, he jumped to his feet and pushed his hands through his hair. He did not look calm. Angela did. Her legs were crossed and one arm was stretched along the top of the couch. I tried to meet her eyes, but she avoided my gaze.

Mom walked over to Cal and gave him a hug.

It seemed like no one knew what to do. The

tension was obvious and the ease that Mom and I had disappeared completely.

"Jes? Can you tell me what happened?" Cal asked quietly.

"Um, well ... I didn't take anything," I said for the hundredth time that day. I looked at Angela.

"Well, neither did I," she said.

I was not planning to turn her in. After all, I hadn't seen her take the necklace. But, I had thought she would tell the truth. It seemed ridiculous now, but that's what I had assumed. How stupid could I be? Really, how stupid? Even I wouldn't have thought I could be this stupid and I was me. I looked at her with my mouth hanging open. And then she did look at me, full in the face.

"It was in your knapsack." She got up regally and left the room.

Mom decided that I should spend the next couple of days at Dad's. I didn't argue. It wasn't until Mom dropped me off that I remembered I hadn't talked to him since he brought me home from the lake. This must be what it felt like to go from the frying pan into the fire.

They talked at the front door while I unpacked my few things. I had clicked the TV on when he came into the room. He reached for the remote control and turned it off, but didn't say anything. He gave me a half-smile and shook his head.

"I didn't —" I began to say.

"I know."

He reached over and took my hand. His was clammy. "During the worst of it with everything going on at home, I made a terrible decision. I had a brief affair with someone at work." His voice faltered, and tears sprang to his eyes. I couldn't say if they fell down his face, because I looked away.

He talked about the woman. She had been a friend. They weren't seeing each other anymore. He said stuff about my mom and me and Alberta. I kept going in and out of listening because it really hurt, but I knew he wasn't trying to hurt me. I just tried to breathe, that's all. Just tried to keep breathing. And even while he spoke — I think he was saying how sorry he was — I thought about what Angela had said on the bus. "Haven't you ever wanted somebody to be a certain way so bad that you pretend they are?"

I guess tears were streaming down my face, because my cheeks felt warm. All I knew was that I hated pretending. Any kind of pretending. I just hated it. So I said, "It's okay, Dad. It's okay."

He took me in his arms then, and he cried like a kid.

20

I was not looking forward to this wedding shower that the now officially psychotic Angela had planned. Everything was lined up for it being a disaster as we hung up streamers and blew up balloons with grim determination. Mom and Cal were still upset, and Angela was pretending that nothing had happened.

The tension was so thick that when Cal asked me to go with him to pick up the cake, I agreed to go along.

"I met the little girl you baby-sit the other day," he said after we'd been driving for a while. "Lucy?"

I nodded.

"Cute kid. She came over to see if you could play. She asked me what my normal blinking speed was," he laughed.

I gave him the kind of smile that requires very little muscle effort.

"Cute kid," he repeated, and he sounded less sure.

Adults usually call the shots, but one trick I know is that when you don't respond to their feeble attempts at conversation, they get nervous. Words are their friends, silence the enemy.

We drove a while longer, and then he summoned up the courage to try again.

"I read a novel the other day."

"Huh," I said.

"I really enjoyed it, too. I think it was the first book I've read for pleasure, you know, that wasn't about my job."

"I thought you only read 'true stories,'" I said, unable to help myself.

"Yeah, well. You got me thinking about that. So I gave it another try. And the thing is, once I got into it … I was hooked. And I realized something."

This time I was firm and remained quiet, but he continued anyway.

"You were right about fiction being about truth, the search for it anyway. I mean, I was totally drawn into the lives of those characters. And, I thought, it's not really any different from what people do in their actual lives. I mean, we all create our own fiction sometimes, don't we?"

Oh, no. Mayday. Mayday. He was turning the simple pleasure of reading into a counseling opportunity.

"We get this one life to live and we turn it into our own story. All the people we meet, in some ways, we create them because we only see them through our own eyes. Someone else might see them entirely differently."

He was speaking quickly now, gesturing with his right hand. Totally into it. "Just drive," I wanted to say.

"And how you respond to every new twist and turn of the plot ... well, it tells you something about yourself, doesn't it?"

"I don't know," I mumbled.

"Well, that's how it was for me. How do you respond to books, Jes?"

Man, he wasn't giving up. And then I was mad. Really mad. Just like that.

"So you read a book, Cal? That doesn't impress me, okay? I'm not my mother. You don't have to get both of us to fall in love with you."

His jaw tightened. I could see the muscles flex, and then there was a very loud silence as he maneuvered the car into a parking space.

As I watched him disappear inside the bakery, I felt ugly inside. And now he would be feeling ugly, too. I knew that. I had managed to create his ugliness. And it was easy.

It was a long, quiet drive home. When we turned onto our street, Cal said, "Your mother and I think it's probably the best thing if Angela goes home after the wedding. Angela agrees." He didn't ask for a response. I didn't offer one. I just tried not to think about how sad he looked when he said it.

I walked to the Kennedys' to see if Lucy was home. Pretty pitiful, I knew — checking on a seven year old to see if she could play. They were just leaving the house, and Lucy raced up the sidewalk. She bounced beside me. "We're going to the zoo," she said, excited. "The actual zoo."

I smiled at the top of her head because she was wrapped around my legs, hugging me. I looked over to her mother. She didn't smile, exactly. But there was a look in her eyes. Just a look.

"To see the animals," she explained.

They got into the car and I could see Lucy waving to me all the way down the block. I waved until the car had turned the corner.

I ended up on the swings at the park. Sam and Dell and I used to live at this park. The slide, the teeter-totter, the merry-go-round, all fit us perfectly. But now I noticed how rusty the chains were, how the red paint was peeling off the bars and that the teeter-totter really did teeter more than it tottered. Had this just happened?

I noticed a couple of little kids eyeing me suspiciously, like maybe I was one of those "strangers" their parents had warned them about.

"C'mon, Dickie, let's go to the swings," one of them yelled as I started to leave.

But I returned and they looked up at me suspiciously.

"Are you Dickie Rathbone?" I asked. After all, how many Dickies could there be in the world?

"Yes," he said.

"Who are you?" The other little boy demanded.

"I'm the voice of the future," I answered, staring him down. He broke first and looked at Dickie, but Lucy's friend seemed unnerved.

"You're only going to meet a few really great friends in your life — boys, girls ... whatever." I looked into his wide, gold-flecked eyes. "Don't squander them."

Dickie smiled uncertainly, and I heard his friend whisper loudly as I left, "What's squander?"

I called back to them. "Look it up. It's a good word."

I almost went to Dell's as I passed by her house on the way home. But I couldn't make my foot take that step. What if she was still mad at me? I couldn't bear to see that look in her eyes.

That was it then. I continued walking down the street. That's how fragile it all was. That's how easy it was to squander love.

"I'm too old for this," Mom muttered as we prepared for the onslaught of women due in five minutes.

"It'll be fine," I said, trying to convince myself as well as her.

Angela came down the stairs wearing a short black skirt and a silky black, see-through blouse.

"Too much?" Angela asked, looking down at her outfit.

"Not enough," I said, walking by with the cheese ball and crackers.

Mom took a deep breath — a cleansing one if her latest reading in meditation techniques was any clue — and answered the first of many knocks on the door.

Within fifteen minutes, the living room was spilling over with women. There were colleagues from her job, neighbors, friends and even a few high-school friends. Amber and Mom squealed when they saw them.

I refilled trays and drinks and took occasional puffs of still-smoldering butts from the ashtrays in the kitchen. Even Mom and Amber had a cigarette when they were outside with their high-school friends, but I think they were trying to hide it.

Through the kitchen window, I found out that Marcy had been divorced twice and had three kids. Jen was still single and had three cats, and Benita was getting married in six months. Mom offered to give her all the telephone numbers and contacts she'd accumulated for her wedding.

"It's what I'm dreading the most," Benita moaned. "All the planning."

"Really? I've had such a good time with it," Mom said.

"You always were so organized ... always had extra pencils in an exam, 'just in case.'"

Mom laughed. "A little obsessive-compulsive, isn't that what you mean?"

The others laughed as well.

"At least I wasn't a tramp," Mom said quite cheerfully, and this set them off into raucous waves of laughter. What were they smoking out there?

I poked my head out the door. "Mom, Mrs. Kennedy's gonna call the cops. You guys are totally out of control."

With hands clasped over faces and shoulders still shaking, they entered the house one by one. I felt like a class monitor.

Only Amber remained outside, still rocking on the porch swing. I could see smoke spiraling up into the night air from her half-smoked cigarette.

"Are you coming?" I asked.

She shook her head. "In a second. The stars are so beautiful tonight."

I grabbed a sweater and sat across from her in a lawn chair.

"It's getting chillier now. Summer's almost over," she said with a shiver.

"Don't say that," I said, looking up at the night sky.

"It'll be back next year," she smiled. Then she took a drag from her cigarette. "Don't tell Sam about this, okay? He'd give me such a hard time."

"Your secret's safe with me," I said, then wondered about the other secret we shared. "You haven't ..."

"He hasn't heard anything from me," she said. Did that mean he didn't know about Marshall and Angela, or that he hadn't found out from Amber?

"But he knows?"

Amber nodded.

"How's he doing?"

She shrugged. "He'll survive."

I knew I shouldn't ask her this but — "Is he mad at me?"

"He didn't say. But even if he is, Jes, he'll get over it. Maybe with a scar or two. But he'll get over it. You can trust him. You know that, don't you?"

"Yeah," I said reluctantly. I could trust him, but could he trust me? I should have told him.

As we sat there, I could hear Angela's voice through the kitchen window, trilling sweetly to one of Mom's friends about how excited she was to be in the wedding, pretending that everything was normal. I could still see the calm look on her face when she looked me straight in the eyes and said she hadn't taken the necklace. I could feel myself stiffen.

"What is it?" Amber asked.

"Angela, she ... it's just complicated," I said. "Everything's gotten complicated."

"She is that," Amber said. "You know, Jes, we all have scars. On the outside or inside. They're the testament that we've lived. Nobody gets through life unmarked."

She gave me this sad smile, and I remembered what she had said about her mom. Probably some scars never healed completely.

She got out of her chair and tapped my head with her hand like she was a really tired fairy godmother and went into the house.

I leaned back on the lawn chair and looked up at the stars. I thought about what Amber had said at the lake, about finding meaning. It was the same thing as those constellations in the astronomy books. It looked pretty clear when the guy with the pencil connected the dots between stars — you could see the lion or the sentry — but when the lines were erased, good luck.

"Hey," Sam's voice came from the gate.

He sat down on the deck beside me. I pulled the sweater close.

"Hey, yourself."

"Dell told me what you said about Angela and Marshall."

Fear twisted inside me.

"She had to go away for the weekend, but she gave me a letter for you." He handed it to me, and I grabbed it eagerly. I tore it open and strained to read it under the patio lights.

Dearest Jes, [a good sign]
Marshall is a creep. A bona fide creep with misogynist tendencies. [Good word, I thought, assuming it was real.] *A pile of roiling rot.* [Yikes, she was back.] *He said Angela came onto him, but who knows the truth? All I know is that I should have believed you. I'm so sorry. Please forgive me.*
Your forever friend
(and so repentent),
Dell

I read the letter twice and then once more for good measure. Each time I felt a little lighter. Then I looked up at Sam's face.

"Why didn't you tell me?"

I tried to read his eyes, but he was in the shadows. "It's not really that much fun to be called a liar," I finally said.

"You didn't think I'd believe you?"

"You mean you would have?"

"I'd have more trouble believing that you would lie to me," he answered.

Relief poured through me.

"What a loser," he said under his breath.

"Pardon?"

"Only two dates and already Angela's cheating on me. Then, of course, there's you. It only took one kiss to freak you out completely."

"You're not a loser, Sam."

"You didn't see your face after I kissed you, Jes. You looked like you'd been bitten by a scorpion."

"That wasn't because of the kiss. It was because it was you."

"Strangely, that doesn't make me feel better."

"It came out wrong," I said. "I meant — I couldn't lose you, Sam. When you kissed me, that's what I was thinking, that if we got together it wouldn't last, and I'd lose my best friend. I didn't think about how I was hurting your feelings. I'm sorry."

"Still, you have to admit I have quite an effect on women."

"It won't always work that way, probably."

"Probably?" He looked grim.

"It definitely won't always work that way — probably."

This time he smiled.

"And you can always call me if it happens again and we'll go up to the lake and fish, or something ..." Even in my ears the words sounded hollow. And young and maybe a little stupid.

"I don't think that's always going to work," he said.

"You're probably right," I admitted.

He looked so much older now with his braces off, and he must have grown a couple of feet during the last few days. Even his shoulders looked broader. Dell was right. He was cute. I opened my mouth to tell him so.

"Good night," I said instead.

He just raised his arm, and then he walked to the back of the yard. I heard the vines rustle as he climbed through the fence.

When I went back into the house, Angela was passing around artichoke dip, smiling and laughing and generally charming everyone. She had a bright smile on her face, but it looked phony to me. Dell's letter had confirmed that she had lied to me, but it didn't make me feel better to know I was right. I remembered what Amber had said about how no one went through life unscarred. I slipped past the crowd of laughing women and went upstairs to my bedroom. I hadn't slept there since I'd gone to my dad's, and even though it had only been a few days, it felt strange ... foreign. I grabbed a pad of paper and a pen and left again. Outside in the hallway, I paused outside of Alberta's room. Taking a deep breath, I went inside.

The air inside the room felt heavy. I walked across to the window and pulled it open. The evening breeze fell into the empty room. All the furniture from when she was alive was gone, but the emptiness was as tangible as the stuff we'd given away.

I sat cross-legged in the rectangular space where the crib had been and began to write. In black felt, I saw words I had not planned make their way onto the page.

THINGS I PRETEND
1) Mom and Dad will get together.
2) Mom and Cal will not get together.
3) Angela will not be my sister.
4) Alberta will come back.

I dropped the pen and stared at those words for a long time.

21

The next day we packed up the cars to bring a bunch of wedding paraphernalia up to the lake. One week to go before "the big day," as Cal put it. Mom and I went in her car, Cal and Angela in his.

Mom didn't bring up Angela's leaving and neither did I.

"Amber said we could use their place if we decide to stay the night. The boys can sleep in a tent."

"Could I stay at Dad's?"

"Of course. He's not there this weekend, is he?"

"He's at Uncle Bob's. He's going to stay there until after the wedding."

We didn't talk for the rest of the trip.

When we got to the clubhouse, I helped unpack stuff. It was an awkward assembly line, everyone carrying boxes, brushing past each other without making eye contact. When we were finished, I took off for the lake.

Sam was taking pictures in the fringe of trees

just above the beach. I walked up behind him. When he saw me, all he said was, "Wait here," and left.

I sat on a mound of grass and dug my toes into the sandy dirt until they were covered to my ankles. I tried to throw a rock into the water but fell short.

"You throw like a girl," a voice called out. Sam was back.

"I'm not even going to respond to that," I said, but I threw the next rock more carefully and it landed with a splash.

I heard a snicker and turned to see Sam holding a scrapbook. He plunked it down on my lap. I looked at him quizzically, but he just raised his eyebrows and nudged the air with his nose. "Look," he was saying.

I opened it gingerly. For some reason my heart sped up. I looked down at page upon page of pictures of me. Me at seven years old, fuzzy, before he'd learned to focus properly. Then at ten, gawky and chubby. Me at thirteen, scowling at yet another incident of Sam popping up from behind a shrub, camera in hand. And me, a profile at the lake with its mauve tranquility providing the backdrop. In the middle of the book was a picture of Sam. It took me by surprise. I must have taken it because his feet were cut off. He was ten or eleven, wearing a really short Amber-special haircut. There was a huge, goofy grin on his face and it made me laugh.

Then more pictures of me. Me smiling, me frowning, me laughing. Me through the eyes of someone who saw. Me.

When I turned to the last page, I could hear my own intake of breath.

It was a picture of Alberta. She was in her stroller, eyes squinting against the sun, making her look older than she was, wiser than she was. Her right arm was raised and her lips were pursed, a perfect rosebud almost ready to burst into bloom. "Onward," she would have been about to say, the only word she knew. My eyes filled with tears, and I looked at the picture for a long time. And then a tear fell beside it, so I closed the book quickly.

"Is it okay that I included a picture of your little sister?"

I nodded, unable to speak. When I could, I said, "Thank you."

He shrugged.

"I'm sorry that it didn't work out with Angela."

"Pffft. No, you're not." He smiled at me, but there was a bit of an "ouch" in the look.

I smiled back sheepishly. "Okay. I'm sorry that you got hurt."

He shook his head and the smile disappeared. "I'm chalking it up to experience." He sounded bitter and it made me mad for him. Mad at Angela.

"She didn't deserve you."

"That is an excellent assessment," he said, picking up his camera. I watched as he focused on a bee hovering above a flower, poised to extract pollen. A sudden click of the shutter told me that he'd seen something more.

"So, Jes. What are we?"

The shift took me by surprise.

"Friends," I said automatically.

"Yes." He clicked again, his camera now pointed to the horizon. I could only guess at what he was seeing. "What else?"

I scanned my brain looking for the right answer. Was there something else?

"I don't know," I admitted.

"So then, what aren't we?"

"Huh?"

"What are we not?" He pronounced the words clearly.

My head was clogged by confusion. "I don't know," I said, exasperated.

"Aha." He spun and turned his camera on me. I didn't look away. The shutter snapped. "So you don't know that we're not more than friends?"

Exasperation melded with amusement and a weird, new feeling of being exactly happy to be where I exactly was. The whole combination made me smile. I heard the click again.

"What was that?" I asked.

"You. Not knowing. Historic, I tell you. Historic." He put the cover back over his lens. "And now I'm off to deliver pictures to Leonard. I'll see you later?"

I nodded, still smiling. To his back I called out, "Thanks for the pictures."

He raised his arm and as I watched him disappear up the path to Leonard's cabin, I had the strangest feeling. It was like a faint shudder, a movement, imperceptible but there all the same, and it was moving me toward something. Silly, maybe. I took a deep breath of Mara air and looked down the beach.

Mom was sitting on the dock. Her back was to me and her feet were dangling in the water. It was a picture that was familiar, but old. It had been years since she'd been up here, like that. I walked down to her.

"Hey, Mom," I said, sitting beside her. "What are you thinking about?"

She didn't answer at first. The purple wind-sock flapped in the breeze above her. Its colors were faded now. I couldn't remember when we'd put it there, only that it was bright and new at one time.

"I was remembering how many times I used to sit here watching you swim. You and Sam ... two little fish ... little silver minnows then." She smiled. "Even if there were a hundred kids out there, I could recognize the shape of your head, the water plastering your hair. You looked like a shining seal. When I'd see you pop through the surface of the water, I was happy. When you dove down again, I'd be concerned when I couldn't see you. It seems so simple now, what made me happy." Her smile quivered, and she had a faraway look in her eyes. I knew she wasn't just thinking about Sam and me.

"Do you still think about her?"

"Every day. And up here even more … I can see her here. She would try to follow you out into the water … how she'd scream when I wouldn't let her go."

My eyes prickled. "Remember how you used to sing to her when you were pregnant? And when you read stories to me, you always patted your stomach, and sometimes you pretended that one of the voices in the story was hers? And Dad would …" I stopped short, not knowing if this was out of bounds since it belonged to the other life.

"What?" she asked.

I breathed. "He would kiss her good night and you would make him do it twice because you couldn't reach. Do you remember that?"

She nodded, and then the tears were loosened and they slipped down her face.

"I do now. But for a long time I didn't. All I could see, all I could remember was the pain. Cal said something to me a while ago. He said if I let go of the pain, it didn't mean I would lose her. That was a big thing for me to understand."

"He helped you do that?"

She nodded. "And once I started loosening up on the pain, or it loosened its hold on me — I'm not sure which — I realized that I was holding on too tight to you. Maybe I thought I could protect you, but I needed to let go of that as well."

"But not completely," I said in a small voice.

"Of course not." Mom looked shocked. "Of course not. Is that how you've been feeling?"

Tears crowded into my eyes and my chest felt shivery. "Kind of."

She put her arms around me. It felt warm and safe. "Oh, never, never, Jes. You are stuck with me."

I leaned into her shoulder. "Amber says that you can only see who someone is when you let go of who you think they should be."

"Well, that's my wise friend. See, for instance …" She sat up straight and looked me in the eyes. "If I hadn't let go of who I thought you were — my perfect daughter who needed constant vigilance — I would never have seen the real you. A runaway, a teller of tales and a felon."

I wiped tears away. "Alleged felon."

"Yes, well. The point is, I've spent most of your life … at least since Alberta died … terrified — trying to make sure nothing bad ever happened to you. But once I stopped being terrified, I realized that you are so much stronger than I thought. And there wasn't a monster waiting in the shadows to take you away from me. I was so scared that day you left and I realized that you weren't with your dad. And I'm not saying you did the right thing, by the way." She gave me a quick scowl. "But you were okay. You did what you needed to do, and I realized you were trying to make sense of your life.

"You know what else I realized? And this came as quite a huge shock to me. I've made a fair number of mistakes in my life. Pretty big ones, and most of them came from trying to be safe. I think that's why marrying Cal feels so right. I've never been so terrified in all my life."

"Huh? You've lost me."

"It's a risk for me to let him into my life. It's not a sure thing. It's a door, I think. And of all the things I want to do as your mother, the most important is to let you see that a person can choose to move forward, even if it scares the hell out of them.

"Your father and I never had an easy time of it. It was always a struggle. That's the truth of it. And you have to know something else. Your father's affair did not cause our break-up. It didn't help," she said, wincing. "But it wasn't the cause."

"Why didn't you tell me, then, about the — affair?" I stumbled over the word.

She didn't answer right away. "I was afraid if I

told you, it would make him the bad guy, and he's not. He's a wonderful man."

I must have looked doubtful. Did wonderful people have affairs?

"He is, Jes. You know that. But he has always suffered ... it's a part of who he is. For a long time I thought I could save him, fix him maybe. But after Alberta's death ..." She rubbed the back of her neck. "I couldn't save us both." She looked at me as though she was studying something.

"Jes, you're proof that we did something right. Alberta was going to be that, too. I can't believe we thought a baby would be our glue, but we did. And when she died, everything —" She wiped her eyes with the sleeve of her shirt. "The light just went out, Jes. And we knew we'd gone as far as we could together. It's just really hard to explain that to your child. I've been telling myself that you would understand this all eventually. That you'd know it was for the best — but how could you? How could you think a divorce could be the best choice?"

"I don't have to, Mom."

She looked at me, not understanding.

"I just needed to know that it was true, that you really couldn't stay together. And I know that now. I can see it."

She put her arm around my shoulders and squeezed, and we just sat there, listening to the wind, watching the shimmer of the sun glint up at us from the water. I looked at the shoreline behind us, the waves from a passing boat lapping against the shining rocks. A little girl in a yellow bathing suit was playing in the sand. I thought of how long it had been the same, all the kids who had played in that water. How it went on and on.

"Alberta wouldn't have been perfect, would she?"

Mom blinked, one eye closed against the glare of the sun. "I suppose not."

"She would have gotten on my nerves, taken stuff from my room, told on me, begged to come along when I went out with my friends."

"You're probably right."

"But Mom ... this whole Angela thing has been really weird for me," I said suddenly.

"I know."

"Yeah, well, maybe you think you know, but I'm not sure. I mean, how could you think she could just waltz in and be my new sister?"

"I didn't, not really."

"Not really? Not at all. Sometimes I actually wonder how you do your job," I said, shaking my head. "Aren't you supposed to understand stuff like this? I mean, she shows up at the bus stop and you don't even tell me, and suddenly she's in my room? My room!"

I was half thinking she might get mad, but she sort of chortled. I didn't really expect a chortle, I'll admit.

"Would it help you to know that most therapists are completely inept at knowing what's going on in their own backyard? We're great in the office. You should see me, Jes; I really have my shit together there. But at home, whew, it's a whole different ball game."

"Your shit together?" This phrase, I have to say, was not exactly momlike.

She nodded vigorously. "It threw me for a loop, let me tell you. I knew Cal had a daughter, but suddenly she was there. Jes, I didn't know what to do. Here I was, scared to death of being a wife again and in walks this ... this ..."

"Goddess?" I supplied.

"Disturbed goddess," she corrected. "If she'd walked into my office, I'd have known what to do. But she walked into my life, Jes. She's Cal's daughter. He barely even knows her, but she's his daughter."

His daughter.

I swear the words jumped out in 3-D when she said them. We were both silent. Angela was Cal's daughter.

We looked at each other, and the look we shared was of instantaneous understanding. No matter what had happened, I was still my father's daughter.

My mom had never ever stood in the way of that. I knew this now with certainty.

"We can't send her back," I said with a sinking feeling.

Mom's eyes were probing, maybe disbelieving.

"Seriously, Mom. When you and Cal get married, she's my stepsister. She's your stepdaughter. But she's his daughter."

"We just thought we should start this thing slowly, Jes. And that maybe she could work things out with her mother first."

"Yeah, well. In my not-so-professional opinion, her mother is a bit of a wacko. Did you know that she told Angela she wished she'd never had her?"

Mom nodded.

"The other day in the department store, when you came in the door, I knew everything would be okay ... even when you didn't totally defend me. It was like, you just know me ... really well. I don't think Angela's mom has a clue who she is."

Mom was starting to get all misty again. I rushed ahead.

"Are you sure?"

I shook my head. "No. It's just a feeling. And I could move into Alberta's room."

She nodded, tears spilling over, and then she hugged me. "You're amazing," she whispered.

After a few minutes, I wrestled free. "You should go tell Cal about your amazing daughter."

Gayle Friesen

"I will," she sniffled. When she got up, she looked about a hundred years younger, and happy. I knew I had something to do with that, and that Leonard was right. You could only ever see someone with a heart of compassion.

I watched her make her way up the shore. Cal was standing on the top of the hill and when she reached him, they embraced. I looked away, but only because it was embarrassing.

Sitting on the wharf with the sun beating down on me, I watched the kids playing in the swimming area. The girl in the yellow bathing suit hugged the edge of the shore, refusing to go any deeper even though her dad was there, coaxing her on. I knew how she felt. She would swim when it was time.

She kept moving toward his arms, and then she'd run back to the safety of the shore. He stood there with his arms open, waiting. Finally she lunged forward and he caught her. Water splashed up in her face and he held her, twirling her around, holding on tight. She laughed, a full-throated giggle that traveled out to where I sat. At the same time, the wind touched my face. It felt like the caress of a chubby hand, and I said good-bye. Because it was time.

22

I woke the next morning with dawn's light and squawking seagulls outside my window. I knew I wouldn't go back to sleep, so I put my bathing suit on. A nice, bracing dip in the lake, that's what I needed. I grabbed a sweatshirt of my dad's — it came down to my knees — and left the cabin.

The lake looked beautiful. A soft mist rose up in patches. Mara's color of choice today was lilac, with spots of navy in the middle.

"But how are you really feeling?" I asked her, and then wondered if this was how crazy started.

I headed down to the dock, prepared to dive into the water, but halfway there I changed my mind. I headed up to the Schmidts' trailer, where Mom and Cal and Angela were staying. I tiptoed past the tent where the boys were sleeping. I knew Angela was sleeping on the cot in the sun porch, so I climbed the stairs and pulled the screen door open. She gave a very undignified snort at the sound, which I found oddly satisfying, but she didn't wake up. I tugged at her foot. This time she woke with a start.

"Huh?" She looked at me blearily, as though she didn't know who I was.

"Come for a ride," I whispered.

"Why?" she asked suspiciously.

"No foul play," I promised.

"My clothes are inside —"

"Just come in your pajamas."

"Why?" she asked again, but she shrugged off the sleeping bag, hugging her flannels around her.

"Just come," I ordered, and to my shock, she obeyed.

We walked down to the S.S. Minnow and put our life jackets on. I told her to sit at the bow, and I pushed us out a little way before climbing carefully inside. Soon we were part of Mara's stillness.

I dipped the paddle into the water and pointed the canoe toward the rope swing. Angela's hands were bundled up in her long sleeves and she sat, huddled and shivering. But the water was smooth and it wasn't too difficult to solo. I was pretty strong, when it came right down to it.

"Why am I here?" she asked, still sleepy-sounding.

I didn't answer right away, mostly because I didn't have an answer.

"Where are you going to dispose of the body?" she finally asked, and I smiled.

"I didn't see the magnetic sticker on the necklace," she continued. "I didn't know the alarm would go off."

"Doesn't matter," I said, paddling harder.

She turned to look at me, and the boat lurched with the sudden movement.

"I wasn't planning to let you take the blame. I just sort of panicked."

This, I thought, was highly unlikely. "It doesn't matter," I said again.

"Yes, it does. It's why you're mad at me. It's why they want me to leave."

"I'm not mad, and I don't think you should go back."

"What?"

"I think you should stay."

"You're lying."

I stopped paddling, and the ripples joined the calm surface of the water almost immediately. It was as smooth as glass this morning, and I could see the lake's bottom, it was so clear.

"You know, when my sister died, I thought it was the worst thing I could ever experience. Then my mom and dad split up and I thought, okay … now it couldn't get worse. Then my mom met your dad and you came into the picture, and I thought you were the perfect daughter for the new, improved family and that maybe it was only me who didn't get to be happy."

"Nobody's perfect," I heard her mutter.

"Well, no kidding. You're actually quite remarkably not perfect, as it turns out. You steal things, you steal people's boyfriends, you lie about stuff —"

"Okay, okay. You made your point. So what? Now you get to be the good daughter?"

"Oh, yuck."

"Well, then, what do you get?" She sounded impatient.

"A sister. That's the truth of it, Angela. And not the evil stepsister kind. Well, maybe a little bit evil," I said. "Yeah. Maybe a little bit."

Angela was glaring at me, but I was on a roll. "But I'm no Cinderella," I heard myself begin to shout. "And I'm not going to sit around in the ashes while you try to steal Prince Charming." Maybe I wasn't making a lot of sense, but it felt good. Plus, I was enjoying the almost fearful look on her face.

"Sam is not a summer boy," I continued. "He's a really amazing person who didn't deserve to be treated the way you treated him."

Angela sat stone-faced.

"And just because you're pretty doesn't mean you can get away with lying to people. I don't even care what your reasons were, because there's no good reason for what you did. We're not stupid. You should tell your dad that you took that necklace because, Angela, he wants to believe in you. He's trying really hard. It's not his fault that things didn't work out with your mom. Or maybe it is. What do I know? The point is, if we're going to be a family, we just have to try a little harder. And that means no stealing, no lying, no batting your stupid eyelashes and sucking up every time you want something. Just get real, okay?"

Wow, it was really quiet after that. I swear, even the birds were looking at each other and saying, "Hmm." The fish, too, probably.

"Have you lost your mind?" She actually said this in a haughty sort of way. She did have style; I had to give her that.

"Yes, I've lost my mind. I've lost trying to make sense of everything."

"Why would I want to stay here with this loony family?"

There was a long pause. Why, indeed?

"Because we are your next best alternative to happily ever after."

She stared at me. I stared at her. I was breathing heavily from my big speech.

Then she stood up.

In a canoe.

The girl was either stupid or trying to upstage me. Either way, the boat tipped and spilled us unceremoniously into the water. I had a strange feeling as I felt the water on my face that Mara was laughing at us. Out loud. A belly laugh.

We both popped to the surface at the same time. We weren't far from shore, so I yelled at her to grab the rope and we managed to haul the canoe to the beach.

We climbed up the shore, soggy and breathing hard, like two beached seals. Angela, particularly, looked a sight with her dripping flannels. I was filled with an overwhelming need to laugh, and I flopped to the sand, giggling. She just glared at me. When I could speak, I sputtered, "Oh, and another thing — you suck at canoeing."

She just stared at me, but then an amazing thing happened, and she smiled, shaking her head. "You're crazy."

I looked up at the path to the rope swing and took a deep breath. "C'mon, before I lose my nerve." I started to climb, and I heard Angela following me up the winding path.

My heart was pounding when I reached the top of the cliff. The sky was pink and a few stars lingered. I was grateful for them.

I took off my sopping sweatshirt and stood in my bathing suit. I took the rope in my hands and climbed to the highest point. After all I'd faced in the last couple of days, I thought the fear wouldn't be here now, but it was, gripping me in the stomach, telling me not to jump. Maybe I wouldn't be able to do it after all. I felt sick with disappointment.

Then I heard Angela say quietly, "You can do this, Jes."

I swiveled on the rock to look at her face, and I could tell she meant it. "If I jump — you'll stay?"

"Maybe," she answered.

I squeezed my eyes shut and felt my body prepare to trust the rope. My feet moved forward, and I followed. I pushed away from solid earth and I was swinging. I heard Angela's voice shouting out, "Now."

I opened my eyes and let go.

The water at Mara waits for me. As my hands leave the rope, there is a moment. In that moment I am suspended. I can feel every particle, every molecule of me. Every thought falls away and every fear. Time disappears and the moment grows wider and wider and wider ... infinitely wider until I'm inside the "Now!"

And, honestly, it feels like forever.